She turned to face her fate.

An intruder, she thought, would have been much easier to handle.

Did *he* have to see her like this? Her pajamas, which had seemed to be making such a statement about the new her—not caring about the opinions of others, eccentric, *free*—now made her feel vulnerable in front of the kind of man a woman did not want to see without her makeup on.

Rick Chase was six feet of utter male appeal. He was tall, broad shouldered, the perfection of an impeccably cut suit accentuating rather than disguising the sleek power of his build.

How was it possible she'd forgotten how handsome he was? Or maybe she'd just refused to think about it, about him.

Because the one thing her battle-scarred emotions did not need was a complication like the one that had just materialized at her front door.

Dear Reader,

I grew up in Calgary, and have a delightful memory of being twelve years old and taking the bus downtown with friends. Naturally, we spent our return bus fare on milk shakes at the Hudson's Bay Company and had to walk home.

An hour or two later, at the halfway point, we made a pit stop at my friend Mary McGuire's grandmother's house, in Calgary's very posh Mount Royal neighborhood, where we were fortified with cookies.

Even now, some thirty-odd years later, I can remember that house. I remember the hardwood floors and the windows, the staircase, a covered porch off one of the upstairs bedrooms, a huge yard. But most of all I remember the *feeling* of that house—gracious and dignified, a witness to the ebb and flow of love and of life. I have been fascinated with old houses ever since, and if I wasn't a writer I would love to have the job Linda Starr has in this book!

I hope you enjoy reading her story as much as I enjoyed writing it!

Cara Colter

A
Vow to
Keep

CARA
COLTER

SILHOUETTE *Romance*®

Published by Silhouette Books

America's Publisher of Contemporary Romance

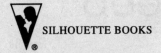

SILHOUETTE BOOKS

ISBN-13: 978-0-373-19842-9
ISBN-10:   0-373-19842-6

A VOW TO KEEP

First North American Publication 2006

Copyright © 2006 by Cara Colter

This edition published by arrangement with Harlequin Books S.A.

® and TM are trademarks of Harlequin Books S.A., used under license.
Trademarks indicated with ® are registered in the United States Patent
and Trademark Office, the Canadian Trade Marks Office and in other
countries.

Visit Silhouette Books at www.eHarlequin.com

Printed in U.S.A.

CARA COLTER

and her real-life hero, Rob, live on an acreage in British Columbia. Their cat, Hunter, graciously shares his house with them. They own seven horses, including two new "babies"—Wiener and Schnitzel, a pair of Fjord cross colts.

Cara Colter on *A Vow To Keep:*

"My partner, Rob, is a building contractor, and he *hates* old houses. The only mysteries they reveal to his pragmatic soul are walls that are out of square and wiring that needs to be redone. A proud new owner of a historic home once asked Rob what he thought the house needed, and Rob looked him straight in the eye and said, 'A match.' I, on the other hand, am a complete romantic and *love* old houses. I think they are our history, and that the walls hold songs and stories."

You can reach Cara at www.cara-colter.com

If you are a fan of Cara's, look for her next story
The Prince and the Nanny
in Harlequin Romance® in March next year.

Dedicated to the people of the city of Calgary

PROLOGUE

THE ringing of the phone was shrill and incessant. Rick Chase startled awake, glanced at his bedside clock. Red digits flashed 4:00 a.m.

No good ever came from a phone ringing in the darkest hours of the night.

He picked up the receiver, aware he was braced for the worst, and hoping for a drunk who had dialed the wrong number.

"Hello?"

"Uncle Rick?"

The last vestiges of sleep were gone. He sat up in bed, the blankets falling away from his naked chest. He fumbled for the light on his night table, as if being able to see would help him hear better.

"Bobbi?"

"Sorry to wake you. I wanted to talk to you before I went to class."

Class? At four in the morning? And then he remembered. His goddaughter was taking her first year of university in Ontario, two thousand miles—and a three-hour time difference—from Calgary.

"Are you okay?" he asked.

"I'm fine." A tremble in her voice said maybe she wasn't.

"What's up, Bo-Bo?" He used her childhood nickname by instinct, knowing it would make her feel safe and listened to, but then he was sorry he had, because it reminded him of her on her tricycle, pigtails flying, days gone that were never coming back. Happy days, uncomplicated.

"I'm worried about my mom," she wailed.

A fist closed around his heart. He was amazed that his voice sounded as calm as it did when he said, "What about your mom? What about Linda?"

"Did you know she sold our house?"

He felt a little ripple of shock. Linda had sold the house? And not gone through his real estate company? His and her late husband's company? It was half *her* company, and she had not used it?

"I didn't know that, no."

"She bought a shack, Uncle Rick, a falling down shack in Bow Water. She e-mailed me a picture of it." She made a gagging noise, Bo-Bo still there, hiding within that oh-so-sophisticated college girl after all.

Bobbi had been raised in the lap of luxury, in a seven thousand square foot Riverdale manor house that backed onto the Elbow River. What she considered a shack and what most people considered a shack were probably two very different things. Still, Bow Water could be a rough neighborhood. Why would Linda, of all people, buy there?

"She's moved in already," Bobbi said, her voice strained with injury. "She didn't even give me a chance to say goodbye to our old house, to pack a few of my own things. She sold the car, too."

"The Mercedes?" Linda couldn't be having financial problems. It was impossible. The company was in excellent health.

"Oh, she still has a Mercedes, but you'll have to see it to believe it." A dramatic sigh, and then, "Uncle Rick, she cut her hair. I think my mom is losing her mind."

He wondered, troubled, if it was a genuine possibility. Linda Starr had survived a terrible tragedy in the loss of her husband thirteen months ago, now her only child was away at school. Could she be falling apart?

No, not Linda, always refined, always composed, always classy. Even in the middle of chaos, she had retained that almost regal refinement, as if she was untouchable, unmovable, a rock that the stormy sea washed around. Linda Starr seemed like the least likely person to be losing her mind.

"What is it you want me to do, Bobbi?"

"Go check on her!" This was said with a certain feminine impatience, as if he was supposed to *know* what to do.

"Okay," he said. "I'll check on her, before work."

From the heavy sigh, a little more was expected of him.

"You need to ask her to come back to work. She's becoming reclusive and weird."

He heard the reproach in her voice and knew it was at least partly deserved. "I've tried to talk to your mother, Bobbi. She doesn't want to talk to me." *Let alone work with me.* Besides, it had been at least fifteen years since Linda'd had any active involvement in the company.

"Give me a break! You could sell snake oil to a rattlesnake farmer, and you can't talk my mother into getting her life back?"

He wanted to deflect the accusation by keeping it light. "Is there such a thing as a rattlesnake farmer?" he asked.

Bobbi was not about to be sidetracked. "You abandoned her after Daddy died. Everybody did."

He wanted to say, *She wanted to be abandoned,* to defend himself, but suddenly his position seemed indefensible.

"And she was so good to you after you went through your divorce from Kathy. Is that seven years ago? Already?"

"Yes."

Another memory, as tender as that of Bobbi on her trike, of her mother taking both his hands in the warmth of hers, looking into his eyes, saying, *It will be all right, Rick. Maybe not today, but someday.*

She had been right, too. When the pain, the humiliation of failure, had subsided, he had realized his divorce had freed him to do all the things he loved. He had bought a motorcycle first, and then, with his appetite for solitary adventures whetted, he had taken up traveling. Not the posh, resort kind of traveling his ex-wife would have enjoyed, but true exploring of a world so rich in diversity and culture he sometimes wondered if he would have time to discover and experience all the things he wanted to.

Still, he knew his contentment with his own lifestyle, combined with the wariness created by his divorce, had made him a solitary soul. Maybe, somewhere in the past seven years, he had even become a selfish, self-centered man.

What other excuse did he have for not being there for a friend? Though, when he thought of Linda, he thought their relationship might be a little more complicated than friendship.

"I'm sorry," he said quietly to her daughter.

"Her whole life was about me, and now I'm gone, too. Uncle Rick, she needs a purpose. Promise me you'll find something at Star Chasers for her to do."

A gauntlet laid down. It would be foolish to pick it up. What did he know about helping a woman whose dignity had been shredded and whose heart had been broken? On the other hand, he knew all about promises. Vows. He didn't want to be that responsible for another human being's happiness, ever again.

"She needs to be around people," her daughter said with the absolute authority of one young enough to still believe she knew everything. "She needs to have something to do. She loves old houses. She still has pictures of some of the early ones that you and her and Dad restored together. That interest could be channeled *constructively,* before she sells off anything else."

He heard himself saying, cautiously, "I can't make your mother do anything she doesn't want to do, Bobbi."

"Promise me you'll try."

Maybe it was the hour of the morning that weakened him, or maybe it was the pleading in that tender young voice.

"Okay. I promise."

"Thank you, Uncle Rick!" There was hope in her voice, as if she truly believed he could *fix* something so desperately fragile. But he already felt regret. He knew he shouldn't get involved in this. Helping someone who was heart weary was like treading on sacred ground.

Still, he'd offer Linda a job, she'd say no and his duty would be done.

But the promise he'd just made implied more than a lackluster effort. That was the problem with promises. They required way more of a man than he was prepared to give.

Dumb to get involved, Rick thought, staring at the phone after he'd hung up, but what if Linda did need something? She would be too proud—and too angry—to ever ask him.

Anger he deserved, he reminded himself, rubbing the last of the sleep from his eyes. Anger he deserved because he had kept her husband Blair's secrets from her.

And he kept one still.

What had he just let himself in for? He got out of bed, went to the kitchen and poured a glass of milk. One thing he knew, he was not going to face Linda Starr without a plan.

CHAPTER ONE

AT FIRST she thought he was not there.

Linda Starr laid low in the long September-gold grass and adjusted the binoculars on the reedy area of bulrushes just beyond the boundary of her picket fence–enclosed backyard.

The ground was gilded silver with frost, but she was only vaguely aware of the cold penetrating her pajamas as the morning light, cool and gray, seeped into the darkness, turned the river's back eddy into a startling strand of light. Across the river, downtown Calgary hummed to life, headlights like strings of moving pearls joined the high-rise reflections in the still waters of this tiny, quiet inlet of the swift moving Bow River.

Unbelievable that she had seen him here, nearly in the heart of the city. It had been a gift, and she realized, resigned, it was one that might not be repeated.

She began to feel the cold and to notice the steady hum of life across the way, in stark contrast to the stillness where she lay shivering. She had turned on the coffeepot before she had come out, and now its scent drifted out her open back door, calling her back to the warmth of the tiny house she had only slept in for three nights.

She rose to her knees, groaned at the stiffness in them and then froze. She saw him, his silhouette that of a ghost taking solid form as the light deepened to rose on the river. Her breath caught in her throat as she witnessed alchemy, dawn turning white feathers to platinum. A whooping crane. Linda had read about him after her first sighting yesterday.

He was one of the rarest North American birds, and the tallest. His wingspan was seven and a half feet. Most people would never see such a bird in their lifetimes. She, startled at her own whimsy, took it as a sign that she had made the right decision to buy the tiny house behind her.

Her knees protested, and she shifted her weight ever so slightly but enough that the bird turned to her suddenly, the brilliant red of his face filling her binoculars, the yellow of his eye defiant. With a buglelike trumpet—*ker-loo, ker-loo*—he stretched his wings so that she could see the black-tipped undersides, witness how truly magnificent he was.

He lifted his wings, and then rose, all power and grace, into a morning sky that had turned a shade of turquoise blue that left her eyes smarting. She could hear the *whoosh* as he claimed the freedom of the heavens. She watched him, felt as if he were setting course for the morning star.

Whimsy, again. Where was that coming from? She had always considered herself so pragmatic. Not, she reminded herself, that a pragmatic woman would have purchased the faintly dilapidated little house behind her.

She kept the binoculars trained on him long after he was just a speck. That's when she became aware of the miracle.

Happiness had eased into her, as sneakily as the morning light had chased away the darkness.

She contemplated the feeling for a moment, let the word roll through her mind. Only thirteen months ago her world had turned upside down, been broken to pieces as if picked up by a tornado and smashed back down. She remembered thinking on that black, black day, *I will never again know joy.*

Or that most dangerous of things, hope.

There was that whimsy again, because spotting the rare bird made her hope for a life where tiny surprises could delight, where cold grass could make her skin tingle with the simple awareness of what it was to be alive.

She had barely formed that thought when the hair on the back of her neck rose. She was aware, before she heard the softly cleared throat, that she was no longer alone in her backyard. Ah well, Linda chastised herself, that was a lesson about believing in happiness that she should've learned. It was like throwing a challenge before the gods, one they seemed all too eager to accept.

The intruder must be a murderer, she decided, just as her daughter had warned her when Linda had insisted on buying this little house, next to the bird sanctuary, in an old, old neighborhood where crumbling houses, such as hers, stood next to in-fills and add-ons and houses lovingly restored to dignity.

Mother. What are you thinking? You'll be murdered in your sleep, Bobbi had said. As if dead bodies littered the quiet streets of one the oldest districts in Calgary. Though, of course, those scruffy young neighbors, tattooed and long haired with the pit bull and boards over their windows, had given Linda pause.

Well, she thought, with faint satisfaction, if her daughter was right about the murderer, at least Linda was not asleep. In her pajamas, though! Heart hammering, ridiculously embarrassed about the pink flannel printed with cartoon devils, she rose off her knees, stretched with what she hoped was a lack of concern—she was sure the criminal element could smell fear—and turned to face her fate.

Her heart stopped.

A murderer, she thought, would have been much easier to handle. She became aware that her pajamas were soaked nearly clean through from the frost, and she was afraid her breasts were probably doing something indecent.

From the cold. Not from him.

At least she hoped the reaction was from the cold. She folded her arms firmly over that area before he got any ideas.

Did *he* have to see her like this?

The pajamas, which had seemed to be making such a statement about the new *her*—not caring about the opinions of others, eccentric, *free*—when she had plucked them off the rack, now made her feel faintly ridiculous and all too vulnerable.

"Rick," she said, hoping to load that single word

with as much frost as what painted her lawn. He flinched, so she knew she had probably succeeded, and wondered why the success gave her so little satisfaction.

Rick Chase was six feet of utter male appeal. He was tall, broad-shouldered, the perfection of an impeccably cut suit, probably Armani, accentuated rather than disguised the sleek power of his build.

Gorgeous, she thought, almost clinically, a man of forty in his absolute prime. His features were masculine and clean, his chin faintly dimpled, those amazing eyes as green as the edges of still water, and just as calm. He was dressed for work—the suit charcoal-gray, the white shirt crisp, the tie silky and classy and perfectly knotted at the swell of his throat.

He was really the kind of man a woman did not want to see without her makeup and her hair done and a dress that turned heads. She reminded herself she had just been *happy* that she had not worn makeup in more than a month, happy with the new her.

Trust a man to wreck happiness without half trying.

She noticed for all the magazine cover perfection of his looks, his dark hair—devil's-food-cake brown—was spiky and uncooperative, still wet from the shower. It wakened some rebel in her that wanted to press down the worst rooster tail, the Dennis-the-Menace one, with her fingertips. She noticed, surprised, there were strands of gray threaded through the rich brown.

How was it possible he was still unmarried, unattached? He had been divorced for more than seven years. And how was it possible she'd forgotten how handsome he was? Or maybe it was just that she had refused to think about it, her battle-scarred emotional self not needing a complication like the one that had just materialized in her yard. Even when he'd left message after message for the past thirteen months, she had refused to conjure the image of him. Somehow she had known it would make her ache. Make her feel as lonely and as pathetic as only a betrayed woman could be.

Betrayed by her husband, now dead thirteen months, and betrayed by this man who stood in front of her, her husband's friend and business partner, who had known about her husband's secrets and had never once…

Don't go there, she ordered herself.

"Linda."

They stood staring at each other as morning deepened around them. Across the river a horn honked and tires squealed.

She was aware of time standing still.

"You look like you're frozen," he finally said.

She resisted the temptation to look down at her chest to see if that's where he was drawing his conclusion.

"What are you doing here?" she asked, not politely, either.

"I called this morning. When I didn't get an answer I decided to drop by."

Drop by, as if this was right on his way to work, which it wasn't. Drop by, as if she had sent him her new address, which she hadn't.

She was a woman who had felt the complete and humiliating sting of being too easily fooled. Now she felt she could sniff out a half-truth at five hundred yards.

"And what exactly is the reason for your sudden concern, Rick?"

Something in his eyes grew very cold, and made her shiver more than her frosty pajamas. She had known Rick for twenty years. Had she ever seen him angry? She was suddenly aware that there were facets to him that were powerful and intriguing, and it felt like a terrible weakness that she was suddenly curious...

"Don't say that as if I haven't been concerned all along," he said with surprising force. "It's you who has chosen not to return my calls. Because I respected that, does not mean I was not thinking about you."

"Well, thank you," she said, her tone deliberately clipped. "And you have chosen not to respect my need for space now, because—?"

He glared at her, raked a hand through the wet tangle of his hair. The Dennis-the-Menace tail popped right back up. He looked very much like he wanted to cross the ground between them, take her shoulders and shake her. But the temper died in his eyes, and he said evenly, "I need your help with something."

Patting down that rooster tail, for one.

"You're asking a woman who is out in her yard in her pajamas at dawn for help with something? You might want to rethink that."

She had said it with mild sarcasm, but he chose not to be offended. Instead he grinned. Oh, she wished he would not have done that. The masculine pull of him was almost instant, more powerfully alluring than before. A smile like his—faintly reckless and unabashedly sexy—could build a bridge right over the painful history that provided such a safe and uncrossable chasm between them.

"I'll take my chances. You never know when you might need the skills of a woman who's handy with binoculars."

She glanced down at the binoculars that hung around her neck.

"So, what were you doing? Spying on the neighbors?"

"In a manner of speaking," she said, fighting down the impulse to explain herself. She was done with that. She was free to watch the birds at dawn if she damn well pleased, and offer explanations to no one. It was the new—and improved—Linda Starr.

"You're shivering." His voice was unexpectedly gentle. Pity? The new and improved Linda Starr did not want his pity; she wanted to be insulted by it. Instead his gentle tone touched the place in her where she least wanted to be touched. The place that said, in the darkness of the night when she could not outrun it, *I want someone to care about me.*

"The coffee is on in the house," she said coolly. "You can come in and tell me what you want."

And no matter what it was, she would say no to him.

She would say no because he was part of a world she was trying desperately to leave behind, and because he made her aware that while she thought she was being independent she probably only looked wildly off balance and possibly pathetic.

She would say no just for practice, and for all the times she had said yes when she hadn't wanted to.

Rick Chase followed Linda toward her house thinking Bobbi really had no idea what she had asked of him. He could tell from the warriorlike pride and anger in Linda's face when she brushed by him that she was going to say no, no matter what he asked.

So, that made his life simple, right? All he could do was try, even Bobbi couldn't expect more than that.

Linda had taken him by complete surprise. She looked astounding, standing outside in her pink pajamas, shivering. She *was* different. Her hair, short now, light brown and terribly misbehaved, scattered around the dainty, defiant features of her face.

The last time he had seen her she had been in black. Her hair had been black, too, pulled into a sophisticated bun at her nape. She had looked elegant, cold and unforgiving.

"Did you know?" she had asked him, her eyes, momentarily vulnerable, pleading for him to say, no, he hadn't known.

He had not answered, and in his lack of an answer, she had known the truth.

His own sense of shame, for being a keeper of the secret—secrets, one that she still did not know about—preventing him from being there for her. Not that he didn't go through the motions. He called. He left messages. But when she didn't return his calls, he did not pursue it. Was relieved not to pursue it.

Still, the difference he saw today was not just in Linda's physical appearance. Before, she had always seemed faintly fragile, now she seemed strong. Before, she had carried herself with a certain remoteness, now she looked engaged. Before she had seemed controlled, now she seemed…was passionate too strong a word?

No.

Who was this new Linda?

He remembered how Bobbi had finished the conversation last night. "I should never have agreed to college, not this year. I better come home. Do you think I should come home?"

Of course he thought she should come home! He certainly didn't want to be the one put in charge of the rescue of Linda Starr, especially since it was now perfectly evident to him she would resent rescue or even the insinuation one was needed.

"Not that I have a home to come home to," Bobbi had announced, faint sulkiness in her tone. "My stuff is in boxes!"

Last night he had taken that as evidence that maybe something was wrong.

But now, standing in the brightening morning, looking at Linda's back, her shoulders set with pride, Rick knew he'd never seen a woman who looked less in need of rescuing. Had he been talked into playing the good Samaritan—used the flimsy excuse of her daughter's stuff in boxes—to come and see her for himself?

Linda, he calculated, was thirty-eight years old.

She had looked ten years older than that at her husband's funeral. Now she looked ten years younger. She looked confident, defiant, madder than hell at being found so vulnerable. And she looked beautiful in a way that threatened a wall he had long ago erected around his life.

His job here was nearly done. He would make Linda an offer. She would refuse. He could report to Bobbi that her mother appeared to be fine. More than fine. On fire with some life force that he had not seen in her before, or at least not for many, many years.

Could he leave now, without making the offer? If he left like this he would be filled with the regret of a challenge only partially completed. His own self-preservation was not the issue here, though he felt the threat of the new Linda strongly.

The issue was if Linda was *really* okay.

She went through the back door of her house, bare feet leaving small prints in the silver grass. He followed them, directly into her kitchen.

He looked at her house with a curiosity he had no right to feel, a spy gathering info. Was it the home of a woman who was doing okay? Or was it the home of a woman secretly going to pieces?

Certainly her house from the outside had been a bit of a shock, had underscored Bobbi's assessment of the situation. Though many of these Bow Water houses were getting million-dollar facelifts, thanks to their close proximity to downtown, Linda's was not one of those. Evaluating houses was his specialty, and hers had no curb-appeal. It was a tiny bungalow, shingle-sided, nearly lost in the tangled vines that had long since overtaken it. It was a long, long way from the gracious manor nestled in the curve of the Elbow River that she had just sold.

Still, the interior smelled headily of coffee and spices he could not identify. Despite the fact that it needed work, it had a certain undeniable cottage charm that suited the Linda with short messy hair and funny flannel pajamas.

She motioned at a chair and poured coffee into a sturdy mug. She slapped the mug down in front of him and left the room in what seemed to be a single motion, leaving him free to inspect for signs of craziness. For Bobbi's benefit? He was kidding himself.

It was obvious she had just moved. Boxes were stacked neatly, labeled Kitchen, waiting to be unpacked. The floor's curling linoleum needed to be replaced and so did the cabinets, the kitchen sink and the appliances. He was willing to bet the neglect was just as obvious in the rest of the house. Still, he could see the place had potential. Possibly original hardwood floors under that badly damaged linoleum, deep windowsills, high ceilings, beautiful wood moldings with that rich, golden patina that only truly old wood had.

She came back into the kitchen. She had tugged a sweatshirt over her pajamas, gray and loose. He was accustomed to women making just a little more effort to impress him, but for some reason he liked it that she hadn't. He liked that somewhere, under the layers of pain, they were still Rick and Linda, comfortable with each other.

The sweatshirt had the odd effect of making her seem very slight, the kind of woman a man could daydream about protecting, if he wasn't careful. A man could remember how, for a moment, when he had told her he had a problem, the wariness had melted from her eyes, briefly replaced with trust.

She got her own coffee, but didn't sit. Instead she stood, rear end braced against the countertop, and regarded him through the steam of her coffee.

Her eyes were brown, like melted chocolate. Once, he had thought, they were the softest eyes in the world. Now they had shades of other things in them. Sorrow. Betrayal. Maturity. But all those things just seemed to make them more expressive and mysterious, the way shadows brought depth to a painting.

Her hair was two shades lighter than her eyes. He realized, slightly shocked, that the black had probably never been her true color. It was as if, before, she had worn a mask, and now the real Linda was beginning to shine through.

"So," she said, "say it. I can tell you're thinking it."

She'd always been perceptive, almost scarily so. He looked at her lips, full, moist and incredibly sensuous. What might they taste like? He hoped she wasn't perceptive enough to gauge that renegade thought!

"Okay," he said, as if he had not thought about the full puffiness of her lips. "It seems like a rough neighborhood."

She cocked her head at him, as if she was politely interested in his opinion, so he rushed on.

"And the house seems, um, like a lot of work for a woman on her own. Why did you sell your Riverdale house for this?"

She took a sip of her coffee, as if debating whether to talk to him at all. Then she sighed. "That house never felt like mine. It was Blair's, his love of status in every cold stone and brick. I hated that house. I especially hated it after the renovation. A glass wall thirty feet high is monstrous. Besides, it was a ridiculous place for a woman alone to live."

Rick hadn't much liked the house after Blair's renovation, either. It had lost its original charm and become pretentious. Still, he had always assumed Blair was solely responsible for the problems between he and his wife. Suddenly it was evident that they had been very different people, their values on a collision course. Linda, more down to earth, wholesome, uncomfortable with Blair's aspirations, his runaway ambition, his defining of success in strictly monetary terms.

Rick didn't want to be exploring the complications of the relationship between Linda and Blair. But he had always known a simple truth: Linda was too deep for his friend. Too good for him. He did not want to be here, in her house, with those thoughts running through his mind.

"Great coffee," he said, wishing he could deflect this awkward moment with a discussion about rich flavor. "What kind is it?"

"I grind my own—several different combinations of beans." Like her daughter, she was not easily deflected. Her eyes asked what she was too polite to, *Why are you here?*

One more question, and still not the one he had come here to ask. "Why didn't you list your house with us? It is your company. Half of it."

Her eyes became shuttered. "I think I've provided quite enough fuel for gossip and speculation at Star Chasers, Rick. I don't want one more single fact about my life to be the conversation at morning coffee, ever."

He wanted to deny that. But he couldn't. Every agent, secretary and file clerk had discussed the scandal surrounding Blair's death incessantly. Each of them had slid Linda slanted looks loaded with sympathy and *knowing* on those rare occasions when business had forced her to come to the office.

He did not know how she had made it through the funeral with such dignity and grace. He did know he did not deserve her forgiveness for his part in the scandal. He did not deserve it because he guarded one of Blair's secrets, still. He felt guilty just standing here with those clear eyes regarding him so strippingly.

Do what you came to do and leave, he ordered himself. Instead he studied the little devils on her pajamas and found himself wanting to know more about the Linda Starr who would wear pajamas like that, outside in her yard at dawn.

"You said you had a problem," she reminded him, still polite.

He tried to think of a problem, but none—aside from the brown of her eyes—came to mind. Thankfully he had made a plan. That's why men made plans, for moments just like this one, when their wits fled them.

He had known he couldn't exactly offer her a job. It would have been unbelievably condescending. She *owned* half the company. What could he say? Come and be senior vice president?

"I'm having problems with a house," he said.

Ah. He saw the flicker of interest in her eyes, and knew, somehow, he had stumbled on just the right way to get to Linda. She loved old houses. The one they were standing in was evidence of that!

"It's an Edwardian, 1912, Mount Royal."

She could barely contain a sigh.

"It's a nightmare." He told her about the water damage, the bad renovations it had suffered over the years, and especially about the daughter of the previous owner who kept coming over, wringing her hands and crying. "She's seventy years old and she laid down in front of the bulldozer when we tried to rip off an add-on porch. Now she has the neighbors signing petitions about everything. I've had two project managers quit."

He had not expected this: that it felt so good to unburden himself.

"And what do you want me to do?"

"Take it over. Be my project manager."

Her mouth fell open. "I can't do that."

"Bail me out, Linda. I made a mistake," he admitted.

"I fell in love with the place. I bought it on pure emotion, never a good thing to do."

Pure emotion, he reminded himself, was always a bad thing. Always. Which is why he had to be very careful around Linda. He felt things he didn't want to feel, even after just being with her for a few minutes.

She turned away from him, and dumped her coffee in the sink, but not before he'd seen the look in her eyes.

Memories.

This was the problem with having come to see her. Their lives intersected and crossed, drifted apart and then intersected again. In her eyes he had seen the memory as clearly as if it had flashed across a video screen.

Him and her and Blair, so young, at the very beginning, buying those horrible old houses, slapping on paint, filling flower boxes, making cosmetic changes and then keeping their fingers crossed when the For Sale sign went up.

"Flip-flop," he remembered out loud. That was what she had called it. Blair had wanted a more sophisticated name for the company, the one they had gotten from combining both their surnames.

She turned from the sink and smiled weakly. In her eyes, he saw yearning. For the way things had once been? For the laughter and excitement of those first few sales? Of those early years?

Bobbi had asked him to help her. More than asked. She had begged him. And Linda still loved these old houses, as much as he did, maybe more. He wanted to walk away from her, for his own self-preservation. But he did not think a man who would walk away from a woman who needed *something* just to protect himself was a man he wanted to be.

"Will you come?" he asked. "At least have a look at the house I've invested your daughter's college fund in?"

What he saw in her eyes was way more powerful than that.

"I don't think I should."

It wasn't the out-and-out no that he'd expected to hear.

"You do still own half the company," he reminded her.

"No, really." She pointed at the unpacked boxes. "I've got a ton of stuff to do. Really."

It was the fact that she said really twice that made him know what she *really* wanted.

"Come," he said softly, foolishly. "Just help me talk to this woman. Look at the house. See if you get a feel for it." He knew if he got Linda over to that house the rest would be a done deal.

"You don't need me," she said.

She was not the only perceptive one. Because in those words he heard how she longed to be needed, how the death of her husband and the departure of her daughter had set her adrift.

Bobbi had been right. He had abandoned Linda when she most needed a friend. It did not make him think highly of himself.

"No," he said. "I don't need you." He wagged his eyebrows devilishly at her. "But I want you."

She laughed, just as he had hoped she would. It was a good sound and a bad one both. It was the kind of sound a man could get addicted to, that could stop him in his tracks when he was way too sure he was doing the right thing.

She threw up her hands in surrender. "Okay," she said, and he could tell the answer shocked and surprised and frightened her nearly as much as it shocked and surprised and frightened him.

CHAPTER TWO

"I'LL have to go change," Linda said, looking down at herself. She could actually feel a blush rising in her cheeks. Her pajamas looked worse for the wear. And the sweatshirt! Why had she picked something that made her look so frumpy and frazzled?

Shock, she realized. She was in shock. That was why she had said yes, she would go look at that house with Rick when it made no sense at all to do that.

Not that her mind was making sense right now.

Rick Chase was having the oddest effect on her. Looking at him—his large frame filling the tininess of her kitchen, his scent, richly masculine and amazingly sensual, filling her senses—she felt her belly do a dizzying drop. She'd known Rick for twenty years. She'd never reacted like this to him before!

Of course, she had never been single and available before.

Available? How did she know that he was? How could he be? Why wouldn't he have been snatched up by someone? He wasn't remarried, but that didn't mean he wasn't involved. It was a different world than the one in which she had gotten married. Marriage was only one choice of many these days. She'd assumed he was alone, but she had learned, the hard way, assumptions were very bad things on which to base decisions.

Bobbi stayed in touch with him, her honorary uncle, her godfather. Would Bobbi have told her about Rick's relationships? Or would she have considered the romantic doings of old fuddy-duddies well outside that small range of things that interested her? Would Linda have heard if Rick was with someone? Suddenly she regretted all those phone calls from people in the office not answered.

"Rick, are you—"

The words stuck in her throat when he looked at her quizzically.

It was none of her business! She didn't care.

"Am I what?"

Don't ask, she pleaded with herself, especially not standing there in devil-embossed pajamas and an oversize sweatshirt. Especially not with her hair going every which way and not a smidgen of makeup on!

"Are you in a, um, relationship?"

There. She'd gone and asked. This was why she had become reclusive. She knew darn well she could not trust herself. Her interest could only be interpreted one way.

"No."

She could feel the blush deepening in her cheeks and she rushed away from him, down the hall and into the safety of her bedroom.

She closed the door and leaned against it, taking a deep, steadying breath. Bobbi had been insinuating lately that Linda was losing her mind. Was she losing her mind? Why was she having this reaction to Rick?

"Because you aren't getting out enough," she scolded herself. So, she would go out with him and look at the house. No doubt after half an hour or so, the hammering of her heart would slow and she would return home more normal than when she had left.

She would, of course, refuse to be project manager on restoring the old house no matter how much she loved it. Then she would make her daily phone call to her daughter, and after that she would make plans to join a club. A bird watching organization might be nice. Perhaps it was time to start thinking about a job, though money wasn't an issue for her.

Just this morning she had felt perfectly content with the challenge of a new house and the occasional whooping crane sighting. Now she realized she needed something that would make her less susceptible the next time she was in close proximity to a good-looking, *available* man.

Meanwhile, she had to erase the impression the pajamas and sweatshirt had made. She did not want Rick thinking she was a pathetic eccentric who had let herself go!

She opened her closet to find very little unpacked. For the last few months she had let the wardrobe thing slide. Especially since her life now belonged to her.

No daughter to wrinkle her nose—*Mom, you aren't really going to wear that are you?*—no husband who she had felt she had been perpetually trying, and failing, to win.

So, she had taken to wearing jeans and workout pants and things that did not match, like an orange T-shirt with red slacks. She had taken to wearing flannel pajamas with pictures on them and furry socks.

Today, the decision of what to wear seemed hard again. The cream-colored slacks and the purple silk blouse the color of a jewel? What was unpacked? Next to nothing? Should she wear earrings? Makeup? Was there any help for the short hair that seemed to do whatever it wanted no matter how she tried to persuade it otherwise?

She drew herself up short. What was she doing? She came to her senses and made a decision.

"Rick?" she called from her bedroom, opening the door a crack.

"Um-hmm?"

"I can't go. Never mind. Thanks for dropping by."

There. What a relief. She sank onto her bed and waited to hear the back door squeak open—it badly needed oil, a much better use for her time than—

There was a faint knock on the bedroom door.

She froze.

The door, still open that crack, slid open further. He stood there, his shoulder braced against the jamb, his thumb hitched through the belt loop of his slacks. His legs looked so long and strong, his shoulders so broad. She *hurt* for things masculine: large hands, whisker-roughened cheeks, easy strength, the sensuous gravel of a deep voice.

She had a renegade thought. She wished he would

come in, push her back on the bed, take her lips with his...which was exactly why she was not going anywhere with him.

She had been putting her life back together, and quite nicely, too. It was obvious he would be a terrible disruption to that process. She looked at his lips. The bottom one was soft and sensual.

A terrible disruption.

"Why not?" he asked. She unglued her eyes from his lips and leaped up from the bed. She pulled a box out of a heap and began to randomly unpack it.

"Why not *what?*" she asked.

"Go look at the house?"

Oh, yes, that.

Whoops! The box she had grabbed was full of underthings! The ones she didn't wear anymore—wisps of lace and temptation. She began to ram them back in the box as quickly as she had taken them out.

"I'm not unpacked. I have to oil the back door. I might bake cookies. A house doesn't feel like home until you've baked cookies in it."

She sounded like an idiot, babbling, but she looked over her shoulder at him and tilted her chin defiantly. Didn't he know he was being rude? He shouldn't be standing there in the doorway of her bedroom *making* her think hot thoughts about him, watching with way too much interest as she unpacked—repacked—her most intimate things.

A little smile tickled his lips.

"Go away," she said, flustered. "I'm busy."

"If you come look at the house, I'll help you unpack later."

Absurd. She did not want him helping her unpack. He was confusing her, bringing a sensation of turmoil to a life that had been without it for some time.

"Maybe not that particular box," he said, and the smile deepened.

Okay, so it would be awfully nice to have someone who could move some of the larger pieces of furniture around. It would be awfully nice to have someone to help, period. But she could hire someone for that! And if she was so starved for things male, she could hire some twenty-something guy with bulging muscles. To look at. Nothing else. Her daughter would be disgusted to know her mother even looked!

Why was she suddenly more aware of being pathetic than she had been since that awful day when she'd learned the truth about her husband?

"No, really, I—"

"And bake cookies," he said. "I'll help you bake cookies."

She turned and faced him and put her hands on her hips. "Rick Chase, you do not know how to bake cookies!"

"You don't know the first thing about what I know how to do."

Now *his* eyes were fastened on her lips with heat. And something else. Longing. Well, that wasn't so surprising, was it? He'd been alone even longer than she had.

But he could have any woman he wanted. She was sure of that.

Weakness flooded her. She wanted to throw herself in his arms, allow herself to be held, to accept the strength he was offering her. But that was the whole thing. She could not be weak. She could not *look* weak. And she would look weak if she did not go look at that stupid house now that she had said she would.

"You were the one who was a lousy cook," he reminded her, his eyes breaking from her lips. "I bet you'd end up with door oil in your cookies."

He was remembering a long, long time ago. Her first efforts in the kitchen, as a new wife and a young mother had been mostly disastrous. But she had applied herself to learning with a fury, and she had become competent enough to turn out items for Bobbi's school functions: decorated cookies on Valentine's Day, chocolate cakes for the bake sale. She had learned how to make lasagna and roast beef and chicken. Once she had even managed to single-handedly cook turkey dinner for Bobbi's Brownie troop of forty-two girls.

But Rick knew none of that. He only knew that Blair, oblivious to her pride in her developing talents, had hired a cook as soon as he could afford one. Roast beef had become Beef Wellington served with Yorkshire pudding, the turkey was smoked and delicately sliced. Linda had dined—often alone—on braised Cornish game hens, slivered Sockeye salmon, soufflés so delicate it was like eating clouds. She felt the familiar cold squeeze in her chest that happened whenever her thoughts turned to her life with Blair. A single thought could ruin a whole day!

She reminded herself, desperately, that now her meals ran to peanut butter on toast with a side dish of quartered tomatoes and that was how she liked it. Then she realized Rick was offering her a morning's respite from those haunting memories and she suddenly wanted to grab his offer with both hands, foolish as that might be in the long term.

"Okay," she said, "I'll be ready in a few minutes."

He gave her a tiny salute and shut the door.

She sank down on her bed. Here was the truth of it: She was, in some part of herself, relieved that her life was being railroaded, relieved that the unexpected was happening, astounded that she was feeling things she had not felt for a very long time. She felt annoyed to be sure, but she also felt alive, in the same glorious way she had felt alive this morning when the crane had lifted itself from the earth.

"Linda," she told herself sourly. "Remember about *happy*. A challenge to the gods."

She found him outside fifteen minutes later. She had opted for the cream slacks, and purple blouse, no makeup, not entirely by choice. She had not been able to find the box it was packed in. Her hair had decided not to cooperate no matter what she tried and was sticking up in rebellious spikes that would have made Bobbi roll her eyes.

Rick was inspecting her car.

"Cute," he said, smiling at her.

She touched her hair self-consciously. *Cute* was not the look she had been trying for at all. *Attractive-but-not-interested* would have summed it up.

Then she realized he meant the car.

It was a Smart Car, the Mercedes Benz developed Micro Compact, another of her change-of-life purchases.

"Bobbi calls it a bean can," she said, and couldn't resist giving her tiny car an affectionate pat. "She can't believe I got rid of the SL-500 for this."

But Linda did not see it that way. She saw it as a step back toward herself, back toward the young woman she had once been who had cared so passionately about her world. She was sick to death of waste, Beef Wellington in the garbage being only one example. She now found excess exhausting. She'd had the dream—the huge house on the river, the staff, the cars, the jewels—and it had drained her energy like a vampire that sucked life blood. She wanted simplicity, she wanted to make her way back to who she genuinely was.

Was the big handsome guy looking at her car going to be a detour on that journey? He looked up, met her eyes. Or did he have the map of how to get where she was going?

"You like it?" he asked of the car, holding open the door of his Escalade for her.

"I love it."

"Good for you."

"And do you like this one?" she asked as he came around to the driver's side and slid in beside her. The vehicle was obviously very nearly new and smelled of leather—and him.

He shrugged, started the vehicle, did up his shoulder belt. "I see it as a necessity, part of the business. I take clients to see properties. I want as safe and reliable and comfortable a ride for them as possible."

She pondered that. He was so different from Blair, who had only been interested in how things looked, how to manipulate people's impressions of *him*. A car like this, for Blair, would never have been about the comfort and safety of his clients.

How dangerous was it that she was comparing Rick to Blair?

"You know me, Linda—"

Did she? That's what she had to keep reminding herself, that maybe she didn't know Rick at all. She remembered those days after Blair's death, when the truth had begun to come out…that feeling of not knowing anyone. Maybe most of all not herself.

"If I wasn't in this business, I'd probably still be driving a motorcycle. I own one. Nothing fancy. I take it out on the odd weekend, head to Banff, or do the ranch country loop through Black Diamond."

Alone? she wanted to ask. But she had already asked that, and it would have seemed way too interested to press further.

They chatted about mutual acquaintances, Rick updating her on the people she had turned her back on. Life, it seemed, had gone on. Babies had been born, couples had married and divorced, parents had died.

She liked the way he drove, with a complete lack of aggression, effortlessly handling the traffic, showing no impatience when things suddenly bottle-necked on Memorial Drive.

"There's the problem," he said.

A young woman stood in front of an older model import, the hood up, staring helplessly at the engine.

Rick signaled and pulled off the road in front of her. "I'll just see if I can give her a hand," he said.

He said it so casually, as if it would be unthinkable not to do the decent thing. A few minutes later, he was back in the car. His hands were dirty and he wiped them on a white handkerchief. He obviously didn't regret his decision, even if it had meant getting his hands dirty.

"That was nice," Linda said, aware she offered the compliment grudgingly. "To stop and help her."

"I couldn't do much. Called a tow truck for her."

It was still nice. Decent. An old-fashioned virtue that she wondered about the existence of from time to time.

"She reminded me of Bobbi," he said. "I'd want to know someone would stop and help Bobbi—or you—if you needed it."

Linda considered her worst weakness to be the tenderness of her heart. She saved that side of herself now for one person and one person only, her daughter. Yet, just now, she was suddenly nearly swamped with a sense of tenderness.

Harshly she pulled herself up. He could have done the decent thing for her once, too. He could have helped her by simply telling her the truth about her husband's affair. He had chosen not to.

That's what she needed to remember when she was getting caught up in the heaven of his scent, in the astonishing green of his eyes, in the way his fingers looked on the steering wheel. She needed not to let those things—or even his chivalrous roadside stop—sway her into believing in the basic decency of the man.

She folded her arms over the place where her heart hurt and glared out the window.

Rick could not help but notice Linda changed abruptly, her thermostat going from just slightly above freezing to flash frozen in the blink of an eye.

What was he doing, anyway? Offering to help her unpack and bake cookies? He was negotiating to get what he wanted, he defended himself. That's what he did for a living. That's what he was good at.

But couldn't he have thought of a trade that did not involve tangling with her quite so personally? He was weaving his life with hers, and that was quite a bit more than he had promised Bobbi he was going to do.

Damn it, he liked her.

He had always liked her. And he had always known, guiltily, she had married a man completely unworthy of her.

He sighed heavily. She glanced at him, and he was afraid she would see his soul, see the weight that was carried there, the burden.

Why had she asked him, earlier, if he was in a relationship? How many reasons could there be for a woman to ask a man that? It suddenly occurred to him that even though he and Linda had known each other since they were both young and foolish, this was brand-new territory for them. For the first time in their shared history, they were both without partners. And he'd offered to bake cookies with her! That was probably akin to a marriage proposal to a widow!

If there was one thing Rick was not doing again, it was marriage. When he'd signed the final divorce papers, he had buried the part of himself that could care that deeply, the part of himself that could be hurt that much.

The truth was, he liked being single. And not for any of the reasons a person might have thought. He did not like playing the field, he did not even particularly like dating. What he liked was freedom: to climb on that motorbike and go without having to answer to anyone or to be back at any given time. He liked being able to phone and book a trip to Taiwan or Bombay or Borneo on a whim. He liked backpacking through Mexico and South America with absolutely no plan, and he liked riding on buses crowded with chickens and mothers and babies and grandmothers. He liked to get up in the middle of the night and play chess on the Internet. Rick Chase *liked* being single!

The *something* that had sizzled through him back there at her house, watching her in her bedroom, could threaten all that, if he let it.

He wasn't going to let it, plain and simple.

She was a good deed, not very unlike stopping to help that girl on the road back there. Linda would probably kill him if she knew. Or perhaps she'd kill him anyway. He slid her a look. He needn't have worried about Linda having designs on him. Whatever he'd said or done back there after he'd pulled back into traffic had sealed his fate. She looked like she'd rather be sharing the car with Attila the Hun than with him.

They entered the Mount Royal area, located on a hill just south of downtown Calgary. Developed between 1904 and 1914, this neighborhood had been developed to be prestigious from the very beginning. The lots were huge, the houses gracious, the boulevards lined with mature, leafy trees. Despite some in-fill housing, the area still held the grace of old money. Houses here started at one and a half million dollars, and many sold for three times that.

They pulled up to the O'Brian house, typical of this area. It had covered porches on both floors, bay windows with original stained glass uppers, wide steps, an enormous yard. Despite the thrill of pleasure Rick felt when he saw the house, he could not stifle a groan. For the one other woman who thought he was Attila the Hun was sitting on the front porch of *his* house, rocking back and forth as if she owned the place.

"There's Mildred," he said. "Careful. She's probably got a shotgun loaded with salt up there on that porch with her."

Mildred, of course, looked like the quintessential little old lady, so Linda gave him a look that branded him an insensitive boor, and bailed out of the Cadillac as if it held a bad smell.

He sighed and got out of the vehicle. He shoved his hands in his pockets and trailed Linda down the walk. Mildred, her face set in battle lines, was coming down the stairs to meet them.

"Linda Starr," he said reluctantly, "Mildred Housewell." What he wanted to say, to Mildred, *was get the hell off my property,* but he didn't want Linda to know just how mean he could be.

"I used to be an O'Brian," Mildred said, laying claim to the house.

"How lovely," Linda said, as if she meant it. She took both the old woman's wrinkled hands in hers. "Would you be kind enough to show me the house?"

Mildred shot him a look loaded with satisfaction, as if she had finally been recognized. "I'd love to," she said.

He unlocked the door. And then he was ignored as the two women explored the house together.

Mildred's granddad had been the first owner of the house, which was built in 1912. Each of the rooms had a story. She knew the history of each of those additions and seemed terribly attached to the worst of the renovations, rooms divided, bathrooms upgraded.

The house was quite terrible inside—original hardwood covered under stained rugs, a distressing life collection of old stuff that no one wanted. There was extensive water damage under the kitchen sink and in one of the upstairs bedrooms, so the whole place smelled musty.

But the bones of the house—stained glass, gorgeous wood, high ceilings, architectural details that no one could afford anymore—were exquisite. Rick knew the Calgary market, and he knew that even if he invested a hundred thousand dollars in restoration costs he could make a lot of money on this house. And restore it to dignity at the same time.

He caught a glimpse of Linda's face, and recognized

what he saw there. Like him, Linda loved houses, plain and simple. Not the new cookie cutter ones, but ones like this, regal old ladies of nearly a hundred who had seen generations come and go, who had character in every line.

"Do you have pictures of the way it used to look?" Linda asked Mildred when they'd arrived back at the front door.

Mildred shot him a look that could only be called vindictive. "Hundreds of them."

"Do you think I could see them?"

"For what purpose?" she asked Linda suspiciously.

"Mildred—" Linda's voice was gentle "—your family sold this house when your mother died."

"But I didn't want to!" Mildred wailed. "How could they do that?"

"I think they knew they couldn't afford to do what needed to be done. Or maybe they weren't interested. It's going to take a great deal of work, but this house deserves to be restored to its original beauty. That's why I'd like to look at the pictures. To get it just right. I'm hoping you'll help me."

Mildred glared at him flintily, as if to say, *See? Someone recognizes my value.*

He wondered if Linda knew what she was getting into, asking that meddlesome old woman to help. But then it occurred to him she was talking as if she was going to do it.

Mildred launched into tales of the house's former grandeur. He felt impatient, but Linda listened, really listened, with the depth and sorrow of one who knew loss. That was what was new about Linda. As she listened to that old lady, leaning forward earnestly, really interested, Rick saw the exquisiteness of her soul. The gentleness.

He could see now just how badly she had been hurt, and not only by Blair, either.

He owed something to her. Bobbi had known that last night when she called. And he knew it now watching Linda. He had helped take something from her, her ability to trust. And he was going to help give it back. He was going to do that even though he knew it would pose a threat to the lifestyle that he enjoyed and to the amount of control he had over his own life and his own world. Because it was the decent and honorable thing to do.

He had not done the decent or honorable thing for all those years, when he had kept Blair's secrets. Nor was he sure, given the opportunity to make the same choice again, what he would do this time. What would he do about the secret he still kept? Would it destroy Linda completely to know the depth of her husband's treachery?

"I'm sure that we won't be able to do everything the way you want it done," Linda told Mildred. "But I want you to know we will cherish the spirit of this house and preserve its dignity. It is going to be absolutely stunning when we are done with it."

Mildred, who had given him nothing but flack, began to cry. This was exactly what she had been waiting for— to know the house would be cherished, some of the memories kept, her family honored.

Rick was staring at Linda. She had known exactly how to address each concern, and she looked at him now with a faint smile. He knew what he and Blair had never been able to give their business. Heart.

He looked into her eyes and saw a place in Linda that he was not sure she saw herself. He saw her soul. And suddenly he knew exactly how to help her win back her confidence in herself, her trust in others that he had, however inadvertently, helped take away.

Mildred left and he and Linda stood looking at the house together. She touched the ancient stones of the wall that circled the property.

"You were brilliant," he said. "Thank you."

She laughed tentatively. "From crazy to brilliant in the space of an hour."

"You're going to do it, aren't you?" he asked softly. He wanted to hold her. Taste her lips, look into her eyes. It was insanity to feel pulled so strongly toward her. It muddied his intentions and made him feel off-kilter. *How could he return her to a place of trust when he kept secrets from her still?*

Maybe she never had to know that final secret.

"What?" she whispered, as if she knew, and as if, should he reach for her in that moment, she would hold him, not slap him. As if their history could be that easily dismissed.

"What?" she asked again.

"You're going to look after the restoration on this house."

Her eyes filmed with tears. He could tell she wanted

to say no. Just as he had been able to tell she wanted to say no to his offer to unpack boxes and bake cookies. But she was helpless against the powerful beauty of that house.

"I'd love to," she said.

Whatever was pulling them together sighed with satisfaction. Would he prove powerless in the face of the powerful beauty he saw, too? Not the beauty in the house, but in her eyes.

CHAPTER THREE

"So, LINDA, can I drop by tonight?"

They had pulled up in front of her house. Rick glanced at his watch.

That small, unconscious gesture reminded Linda, poignantly, that she was not a busy person with places to go. Her daughter had been her reason to get up in the morning, and now her daughter was three thousand miles away and Linda's life, at times, seemed unbearably empty, without a purpose. But she reminded herself that just this morning, the whooping crane had seemed enough! Her small house had seemed enough. Wasn't it just like a man to awaken sleeping dissatisfactions? Besides, now that she had agreed to take on the O'Brian project, everything in her life was about to change.

She did not want Rick to go. She liked the time they had spent together. Watching whooping cranes at dawn was not going to be enough to soothe the loneliness in her—the loneliness that she had been almost completely unaware of until he had appeared in her backyard.

Even before the death of her husband, she had made

Bobbi her whole world. She had sewn Halloween costumes and been president of the PTA. She had driven to music and skating lessons, the dentist, the doctor, the optometrist, the orthodontist. This last year, when Bobbi had been too old to need mothering, Linda's world had revolved around finding the perfect prom dress and planning the perfect graduation celebrations. Her world had been about finding funny little notes and gifts to put in her daughter's lunches. The last year had been about time just for them—popcorn and movies and shopping sprees. Linda had been almost desperately aware of the clock ticking.

Had she used her daughter as an excuse, becoming almost reclusive in her reluctance to reach out to people or to accept their reaching out to her? Had she become lonely and pathetic? Well, even if she had, Linda was determined not to look that way!

"Tonight? I'm sorry, Rick, I have plans."

He raised an eyebrow, inviting her to share confidences with him. But she'd rather leave him contemplating the possibility that she had a big date. Her plans were nothing very exciting—scrubbing the old tub until it shone, unpacking the kitchen boxes. But he didn't have to know that!

"Okay. How about tomorrow night then? I'll drop off the budget and a directory of my favorite contractors. Do you think you'll want to go payroll or percentage?"

She knew taking a percentage would be a bigger risk. That was one of her brand-new goals: to take bigger risks.

"Percentage," she said without hesitation, and he gave her a nod of approval.

Oh. She felt incredibly foolish. Suddenly Linda realized she had another new goal. She didn't want to play games with Rick. It was too much like her marriage—a chess game of moves and counter moves that never produced anything close to intimacy. The new and improved Linda Starr was not going to play games designed to manipulate people's impressions of her. She was scrubbing a tub tonight. That was her real life, and somehow it seemed very, very important to her that she always be one hundred percent real with Rick.

Besides, Rick offering to bring the information to her was a blessing. She wouldn't have to face the knowing looks of people at the office. Is that why he'd offered to do it? To spare her embarrassment or awkwardness?

"Actually, Rick, why don't you drop by tonight? The things I had planned aren't so urgent they can't wait." She took a deep breath. "Scrubbing the tub, actually."

If he found her plans in the least pathetic, nothing in his handsome features said that. He looked genuinely pleased. "Great. The sooner we can get up and running on this house, the better. I'll see you at eight-thirty. That's not too late is it?"

Oh, great. Now that he knew her big plan was to scrub a tub, he thought she was in bed with a good book by eight-thirty? Not that the idea was totally inaccurate on some nights!

"No, that's fine."

She got out of his car, and he drove away. She watched him go, then turned slowly back to her house. Her whole life had taken a new direction since she had spotted that crane this morning. She was not all that unhappy about it.

"Oh, Linda," she said out loud to herself as she let herself in her door, "you are dancing with danger."

She sighed. She had so much to do here. She wanted to paint and refinish the floors. She wasn't even finished unpacking! What was she thinking taking on another commitment? She was thinking she might have a life again, rich and purposeful, bigger than the small safe world she had wanted when she had bought this house.

"This is going to be good for you," she told herself with determination.

Then, even though she knew unpacking her kitchen things should be her priority, she went right to her bedroom and began rummaging through those boxes. She unearthed perfume and makeup, a soft white angora sweater, black slacks and a set of tiny diamond earrings and a matching tennis bracelet. Then, as if she didn't have dozens of urgent things to do in her new home, she tried on the outfit. The image was just right. Soft, sexy in an understated way, professional.

"Now whose impressions are you trying to manipulate?" she asked the mirror sternly.

She wasn't trying to manipulate impressions! She just wanted to look her best—to wipe the memory of fuzzy pink pajamas from Rick's mind. There was nothing wrong with a woman trying to look her best. Even if it had been more than a year since she had made any effort. Maybe especially when she had neglected herself for too long.

The outfit selected, Linda spent the remainder of the day unpacking boxes. She even found time to scrub that tub. Then she showered, changed into her selected outfit and coaxed her hair into some semblance of order. She sprayed perfume, just a subtle hint, and subtle was her mantra when applying makeup, too.

Though when regarding herself in the mirror, as makeup application required, she noticed signs of age: delicate crows-feet fanning out around her eyes, a faint "worry" wrinkle becoming permanent in her brow, the line of her jaw becoming less pronounced. Perhaps it was awareness of those defects that made her so nervous as eight-thirty approached, like a teenager waiting for her date to arrive.

"Ridiculous," she told herself. "It's Rick!" A man she had known forever, for all her adult life. How foolish to feel in any way anxious about his arrival.

Still, she did. In fact she felt almost giddy with nerves when she opened the front door to him at twenty minutes after eight. Punctual, she thought with approval, just as if she was evaluating him, assessing his potential.

For what? she chided herself, but she knew. *For the future.*

Her annoyance with herself for being so absolutely juvenile did not bring an end to the evaluation. When she looked closely, he too was showing signs of age: squint lines around his eyes that seemed to draw attention to the thick sooty abundance of his lashes, silver threaded through the darkness of his hair that made it seem more tantalizingly touchable. Why did maturity look so good on some men? Rick was in jeans and a casual long-sleeved shirt in a shade of forest-green that made his eyes look absolutely stunning. He had shaved and his hair was freshly combed, but she couldn't help but notice the rooster tail sprang free of his attempts to tame it. Her fingers itched to soothe it, and she shoved her hands behind her back and locked her fingers together.

"Hi," she said, and was pleased that her voice sounded completely normal, not the voice of a woman thinking renegade thoughts about the future or taming hair.

"Brought you a present," he said, juggling his brief-case in one hand and a bag in the other.

"A present?" She stepped back and let him by. "What for?"

"House warming," he said enigmatically.

"You didn't have to do that!" But she was secretly glad he had!

She had cleared most of the boxes out of the living room so they could sit in there, but Rick glanced around and made his way right through it to the kitchen. Damn. Making himself at home already!

He set his briefcase on the floor, and the bag on the table. He began to empty the bag.

She laughed out loud. He presented her with three sausagelike rolls of premade cookie dough.

"Chocolate chip, chocolate chunk pecan and oatmeal raisin," he announced. "I told you I knew how to make cookies. Which one?"

"Chocolate chunk pecan, of course."

"I knew you'd say that."

"You did? How?"

"I just had you pegged for a chocolate chunk pecan kind of girl."

It had been a long time since anyone had called her a girl. She had a feeling the politically correct thing to do would be to tell him girlhood was many years—and bad experiences—behind her. But she didn't.

"Also—" he reached into the bag and brought out a box "—chocolate fudge brownies, with frosting. That should get your house smelling like a home."

"I still vote for chocolate chunk."

"I knew it," he said with satisfaction. "We can save the brownies for next time."

We. Next time.

This was where the real danger lie, not in the fact that she had accepted a new job, but in the fact that she had accepted him back into her life.

But if he sensed her sudden uneasiness, he did not let it show. "And," he said, "I brought you this!"

With flourish, he brought out a canister of tub and tile industrial-strength cleaner.

She was ridiculously touched by the gesture. He had actually listened to her!

She took the canister and hugged it to her. "Thanks," she said. "I have a wonderful Saturday night planned now."

Something in his eyes went smoky. "Oh?" he said. "Bubbles? Candles?"

She found herself blushing. "I meant I was going to spend my Saturday night cleaning the tub!"

"Well, no woman is so obsessed with clean tubs without a reason," he said.

She couldn't speak. This discussion of bathtubs and candles and bubbles with Rick was enticingly intimate. And what was that look in his eye? As if he would join her?

She must have been mistaken, because he turned from her abruptly.

"Cookie sheet?" he requested. "We can bake them, and go over the material on the O'Brian house while we wait."

"Multitasker." She tried for a teasing tone, but her mind was still on bathtubs.

"Oh, yeah."

How could this be so easy, and so hard at the same time? He was making her feel flustered and gauche, like a young girl who knew nothing of men, instead of like a thirty-eight-year-old woman who had buried her husband, who had a daughter in college, who had just bought her first house and her first car all on her own.

She unearthed a cookie sheet from one of the boxes.

"Now watch," he said sternly. He peeled the plastic off the cookie dough roll, removed a generous glob with his fingers and pasted it on the cookie sheet. Then he took a wooden spoon and smashed the dough robustly. His cookie took up approximately an eighth of the cookie sheet.

She laughed.

He glared at her. "It's no laughing matter. Making the perfect cookie is science."

"Your method just seems, er, very masculine."

"Well, let's see yours, then," he challenged her.

She retrieved a spoon, removed a small amount of dough from the wrapper, shaped it into a perfect ball and placed it on the cookie sheet without having once touched it with her fingers.

"Do you object to fingers?" he asked. And then he licked some of the cookie dough right off the tips of his!

How could anyone object to fingers when they looked so, er, tasty?

"No," she stammered, "I don't object to your fingers."

"Well, I don't object to yours, either."

She shaped the next cookie with her hands and licked the dough off. It felt wonderful not to be Ms. Perfect getting ready for the school bake sale!

They stood side by side at the counter plunking dough onto the cookie sheet. The activity seemed intimate and cozy, like something a family might do together.

Hadn't she, once upon a time, had chocolate chip cookie dreams for her family? But Blair had not. Making cookies or Sunday morning pancakes would never have been his idea of a good time. He had made that clear when she'd found herself pregnant. He'd married her, even though that had not been in his immediate plans. He'd done the honorable thing, even though he was not a domestic kind of guy. Frightened and starry-eyed all at the same time, Linda had made the age-old error of thinking he would change his mind. Instead she had spent way too many years trying to make up for the fact that he had been trapped in a lifestyle he didn't want.

Now, she felt angry just thinking about it! That ache started in her chest—

"Hey!" Rick took the wooden spoon that he had been using to flatten cookies and pressed it against the bridge of her nose. "It's only cookies! Don't look so intense. You'll get a wrinkle!"

The spoon was pressed against the very place where she had spotted that wrinkle making itself at home on her forehead! With as much dignity as she could manage she said, "At my age I've accepted wrinkles as a fact of life. New one every morning."

"Really?" He looked at her face intently. And then he said softly. "I have to say I didn't notice that. I thought you looked very beautiful. As beautiful as I have ever seen you look."

They both went very still. For a horrible moment she thought she was going to cry. It had been so long since anyone had called her beautiful. So very, very long.

Then he frowned slightly. "Whoops, I got dough right here."

He reached out with his finger and scraped a dab of dough from her forehead. Then he put it in his mouth.

She felt as if she might stop breathing. The moment had come from nowhere, the tenderness of his touch, coupled with the knowledge that he found her beautiful, nearly blinded her.

"Okay," she said, before she started to cry, or did something else foolish. She grabbed the spoon from him and flattened an unsuspecting cookie, "Let's get these in the oven and then get down to business."

Then she flushed furiously, as if the business she had in mind had nothing to do with that briefcase over there.

"You have cookie dough on your sweater," he said. Was his voice a little hoarse?

She looked down at her sweater. The awareness of the heat sizzling in the air between them intensified. Okay, if he rescued *that* dab of dough, she was going to be lost.

But, thankfully, he didn't.

He whirled from her, and while she opened the oven door and let the heat bathe her face—an excuse for the color there—he settled at the table and emptied papers out of his briefcase.

After she had discreetly cleaned the cookie dough off her sweater she joined him at the table.

"Okay," he said, determined to be all business, "this is what we paid for the house."

Determined to be all business, too, she looked at the figure. "A deal for that neighborhood," she said.

"That's my job. I find the deals. I look for what everyone else is missing."

"Others held their noses and saw the mess and the work," she guessed, "you saw the bones." He was good at seeing bones. It seemed he had seen hers, too. Despite what the years had left on her face, he had seen something else. Beauty. She was finding it hard to concentrate.

"Exactly. So, this is my estimated budget for demolition and restoration."

He passed her a neat piece of paper.

She looked at the figure printed there and gulped. "This is a lot of money, Rick," she said uncertainly. "And I haven't done this kind of thing for a lot of years…"

"You can do it," he said.

"How do you know?"

"I can see it in your face."

Again, she had to fight that awful impulse to cry. Why was he doing this to her? Seeing things in her like beauty and strength and talent that no one had seen for such a long time? And why did his belief that she possessed those qualities make her so sure that she did, too?

"This is what I think we can sell the house for, when we're done."

She stared at the figure, did a little silent math.

"My daughter's college fund is safe with you, isn't it?"

He laughed. "Well, there's a lot of variables between figure number one and figure number three. It's a best case scenario."

Linda realized she had become one of those variables. He saw her as beautiful and strong and skilled, but what if she wasn't? She felt scared. Of trying. Of not doing well. Of failing. But then she realized the house was beautiful and strong, too, and it needed exactly the right person to uncover its full glory.

She was that person.

Was he going to be that person for her?

Rick, apparently oblivious to the momentousness of the discovery she was making, was showing her a pamphlet from a man who specialized in old flooring.

"Look at this," he said with a tone that was almost reverent. "He harvests boards from old barns and refinishes the wood."

Linda's doubts dissolved as they went over the list

of tried-and-true contractors Rick had been working with for a dozen or more years.

She began to feel excitement.

The stove bell rang.

Rick put the papers aside. "I'll leave all this with you. Taste test time. No, sit. I'm in charge. Presentation is everything in this business."

Old houses or cookies, he knew how to do it. He found a plate and presented his huge misshapen cookie to her. She took a bite and declared it delicious. He took one, too, from the same cookie. She wasn't quite sure why it was sexy that they were eating the same cookie, but it was!

Then they sampled her perfectly round cookie.

"Not as good," he declared solemnly. "Too perfect."

She took a bite of the perfect cookie he offered her. How could two cookies made from the same dough on the same cookie sheet in the same oven taste totally different?

"Agreed," she said. "Cookie number one is the winner."

Then they ate cookies, one after another until she felt almost delirious.

Since his divorce, Rick had been bitten by the travel bug. He had smelled jasmine in Jordan, spices in the open markets of India, roses in English gardens. But, sitting there in Linda's humble kitchen, Rick was not certain he had ever smelled anything as exotic, as enticing, as the sweet fresh scent of her soap mixed with cookies baking in the oven.

He glanced at her now, looking earnestly over the

budget for her project, and it was as if he was transported back over twenty years. The look in her eyes was the look of a young woman—eager, scared, brave, ready. Yet her face had matured in ways that made her more beautiful than she had ever been before. He had meant it when he had said that to her.

She got up to take the second tray of cookies out of the oven, and he snuck a good long look at her.

The sweater, he was sure she would be horrified to know, reminded him of the pajamas he had found her in this morning. Oh, the sweater was much more sophisticated, and molded her soft curves instead of hiding them, but both items of clothing seemed so infinitely touchable, made her seem so appealing, a woman made to be gathered in a man's arms.

"Here." She set the fresh platter of cookies in front of them.

He reached for one, even though he'd had more than enough, and bit into it. It was ambrosia. He had to close his eyes against the sensation of the hot cookie melting on his tongue.

He had eaten some of the best and most exotic foods in the world. How could it be that a simple cookie—not even honestly homemade—could be doing this to him?

He opened his eyes. She sat across from him, her eyes closed in pleasure, a little smear of melted chocolate chip on her lip. If something didn't happen, he was going to have to do something about that chocolate chip.

But something did happen.

The phone rang.

She got up and looked at her caller ID with pleasure.

"Bobbi," she mouthed, picking up the phone.

It occurred to him as he watched her changing facial expressions, as she shot him a look and said in a clipped tone, *is that right,* that maybe he should have called Bobbi himself. Just to let her know he'd let her mother think his approaching her had been his idea. The look on her face said there would be no removing of melted chocolate from her lips anywhere in his near future.

She hung up the phone. She crossed her arms over her chest and glared at him.

"Cookie?" he said uneasily.

"This was all Bobbi's idea?" she said with heat. "You dropped by this morning at her suggestion? Offered me a job because my daughter was worried about me?"

"Well," he said uneasily, "yes and no."

"You might want to clarify that."

"Yes, I might. I mean she did call me. She was worried. About the sale of your Riverdale house, your choice of a new car. She did ask me to check in on you."

"Take your cookies and your brownies and get out of my house."

"Now, Linda."

"Don't you 'now Linda' me, you scoundrel!"

He should have been feeling terribly awkward. Instead he felt rather in awe. Linda, angry, was incredible. Her eyes were sparking and her chest was heaving. Unless he was mistaken she was going to throw something.

She did.

She picked up a freshly baked cookie and hurled it at his head. He ducked and it whistled harmlessly by him.

"You came here because you pitied me?"

His gaze locked on her, he could not really remember why he had come. Certainly, at this moment, she was not a woman a man would ever couple with the word "pity."

"If that is why I came—"

Another cookie whistled by his head. "— it's not why I'm here now."

She had picked up another cookie, and she hesitated.

He rushed on. "Linda, when I saw you in that house, I just knew it was a perfect match. Like chocolate chunks and pecans."

"Get out."

"Not until we resolve this maturely."

"I don't want to resolve it," she said.

In the way she said it, he suddenly saw how very vulnerable she was. She thought, he could see it in her eyes, that he had come to her in pity, found her pathetic, made a work project for her.

He knew of only one way to make her understand, beyond a shadow of a doubt, that he did not find her pathetic.

Not at all.

He crossed the distance between them.

"What are you doing?" she asked. She held up that cookie as if it was a laser pistol. "Stay back."

"No," he said, and moved one step closer.

She retreated one step, and it was all the retreat her tiny kitchen would allow. The wall was at her back.

"You have some chocolate right here." He touched her lip.

She did not flinch, or duck her head to move away. She looked at him with eyes that begged him to show her why he was here. Not because he pitied her. Not because she was pathetic. But because she was irresistible. More beautiful than she had been in her entire life. He moved his finger from her lip to his mouth.

Her eyes widened and her mouth formed the most adorable "O."

He tasted the chocolate, but it was not the taste he craved. He leaned forward, and touched his lips to hers.

It was not until he tasted her that he realized he had wanted to do this for more than twenty years, had lived for this, had prayed for it. The strength of what that tiny meeting of lips had done to him, made him reel back from her, astonished.

There was the astonishment of discovery in her eyes, too.

"Well," she said. "Well."

She reached up with the hand that was not still holding the cookie. He thought she was going to wipe his kiss from her lips, but she didn't. She touched the place his lips had touched, her eyes luminous.

"I guess I should go," he said, when he wanted nothing more in the world than to stay. His mind—male, undisciplined—drifted to thoughts of bathtubs. Bubbles. Candles.

"I guess you should," she agreed, but not with conviction.

He backed away from her, from the thing that shivered in the air between them, like electricity on a hot summer night before a storm.

"I need you," he said, and then realized that had come out wrong. "I mean the O'Brian house needs you. Really."

She nodded.

"So, you'll still do it?"

She nodded again, a woman in a trance.

"All right then." He retreated to the table and started stuffing papers in his briefcase, trying to remember what he needed to leave here with her and what he needed to take. He turned, afraid if he looked into her eyes again, he was not going to be able to control himself. He would drop the briefcase and cross the room, plunder the softness of her lips like a buccaneer on a pirate ship.

A buccaneer on a pirate ship? He chided himself. Rick, snap out of it.

"Good night," he said and went quickly for the door. His hand was on the knob when her voice stopped him.

"Rick?"

He turned and looked at her.

"Thank you."

Then she blushed and added hastily, "For the cookies."

But they both knew that was not what she meant, and he knew it would be tempting the gods to tell her she was welcome.

Because both of them would know he did not mean she was welcome to cookies.

CHAPTER FOUR

RICK got in the door of his upscale Eau Claire condo and took a deep, relieved breath, as if he was a man who had just snaked his way through a minefield and somehow survived. He'd been so distracted on the way home, he had nearly rear-ended the vehicle in front of him when it stopped suddenly.

He had kissed Linda Starr, touched his lips to hers. The kiss had been light and quick, yet it had given him a glimpse of something *missing* in himself. It had rattled him far more than such a brief experience had any right to do!

He turned on the entryway light, and it spilled brightness into his sanctuary. He entered the living room, his favorite of spaces, and looked around with faint desperation, wanting his things to ground him, to pull him back into his world.

His distressed leather sofa and armchair were large and masculine, as solid as he had been before he had gone to Linda's tonight. Throughout the room were remembrances of his many travels—the hand-carved giraffe from Africa, a silk-covered settee from India, a Persian area rug that he'd bartered for at a market in Turkey, a silver pewter mug from the Abby in London.

His *stuff*. It had always made him feel rich and contented. Full. Yet tonight, when he had kissed Linda, it was as if everything that had come before had been pure illusion. A man could not fill his soul with material possessions. They could not touch the place in his heart that Rick had suddenly discovered was shockingly empty.

In a last ditch effort to outrun what he had just discovered about himself—that he was a deeply lonely man—Rick touched the rich carved wood of a wooden trunk he had acquired in China. He felt nothing.

The air in his home smelled of nothing, sterile, and he wanted it to smell like chocolate chip cookies. He glanced at the clock. It was not too late to visit the nearby late-hour supermarket. He could make cookies himself. He could fill his house with rich aromas himself. He didn't need *her*.

He opened the doors on the cabinet that disguised his TV and sank onto his sofa. He flipped furiously through channels before he realized he could not outrun what he wanted to outrun with mindless programs, any more than he could outrun it by admiring his possessions.

He had kissed Linda Starr.

When his lips had touched hers, it had felt as though he had waited his whole life for that moment. Every other thing—every travel, every collectible, every achievement, every house—paled in comparison. Every fleeting moment of joy and every encounter with hardship had suddenly become trivial and insignificant. In the darkness of Linda's eyes, in the softness of her lips, he had glimpsed the one place he had not yet traveled to. The foreign land that was his own heart.

He turned off the TV, sat back and closed his eyes. "Shoot," he said softly.

He had set out to prove to her that he had not come to her with his job offer out of pity. He had set out to prove to her that he did not find her lonely or pathetic. But he had only proved that he did not truly know himself.

He was lonely. *He* was pathetic. He had traveled the world trying to fill the holes in his heart with experiences and collectibles.

"Enough," he snapped at himself and leaped from the chair. He'd go get those cookies from the store, after all. The scent, the rich sweetness of chocolate melting on his tongue, had drugged him somehow. He could have that drug in the safe confines of his own world.

But an hour later, removing cookies burned nearly black from his oven, he knew he was kidding himself if he thought cookies were going to do it for him. It wasn't the scent of cookies he wanted. It was the scent of her, intoxicatingly feminine, tantalizingly sensual, that he wanted. The strength of that desire—his sense that nothing else could now fill that place within him—unnerved him and made him stubbornly try to regain his old world, where he was in control.

"I have to stay away from her," he vowed. He had to not think of her. At all. Not of melted chocolate on her lips or the melted chocolate of her eyes. Certainly not of the *scent* of her, like spring breezes coming after a long, hard winter, carrying promises.

Work, he ordered himself. It had always been his balm. When it had become apparent that his marriage was over, when he had left it for good, he had thrown himself into work, become a man possessed. How many houses had he purchased and flipped in those years following the divorce? Dozens? Hundreds?

Now he opened his briefcase, eager for the respite work could give him from his thoughts. Laying right on top were all the things Linda would need to get started—contractor's phone numbers, budget numbers, glossy pamphlets from favored suppliers.

"Shoot," he said again and ran a hand through hair already thoroughly mussed. Now he had no choice about seeing her again.

He'd drop off all these things for her tomorrow, at the O'Brian house, not at her cluttered cookie-smelling cottage. That seemed like a magic place now, where a man could be lured by things so sweet he could not even contemplate them without becoming enchanted.

Even better, he would get someone from the office to drop off these things.

He stuffed the papers back in his briefcase, went to his upstairs office and flicked on his computer. A message from Bobbi. *Thank you!*

He groaned and shut off the computer without looking at his other messages. He crossed the hallway to his bedroom, a loft-style room that looked over his living room on one side and had a wall of windows on the other. The windows faced the river, and he contemplated the water's inky mystery for a long time, before finally going to bed.

A bed that was way too large for one man, alone. He knew he was going to toss and turn and think endlessly about how his well-ordered life had been disrupted in the space of less than twenty-four hours.

In the space of less than five seconds, lips brushing lips…

He crawled between the fresh linens and tried to make himself focus on going to Bali over Christmas.

Instead he thought about what she'd said. She didn't want to see anyone from the office. She felt humiliated by what they know about her life. So, it wouldn't be fair, it would be insensitive, to have someone from the office deliver the papers.

So, no big deal. A courier, then.

With that settled, he began to imagine walking on a white sand beach, the water turquoise, the palms swaying in a gentle breeze. Then, somehow, Linda was there, too, her hand in his.

A courier would not be delivering anything to her, at least not from him.

That decision made, Rick slept instantly.

In the morning, though, he found he was not quite as brave as he wanted to be. Her and him and her lips alone in that big house was just too much temptation. He had a responsibility to start this thing off as he meant for it to go. And that did not, unfortunately, include making himself susceptible to Linda's lips.

He called his favorite contractor, an ambitious and brilliant young guy named Jason, and asked him to meet him at the O'Brian house.

"Can't do it this morning," Jason said emphatically.

"It has to be this morning," Rick said, just as emphatically.

"What's the sudden rush?" Jason asked.

"I've been burning daylight on this one a little too long. Besides, I want you to meet my new project manager."

He and Jason had done at least a million dollars' worth of business together. He didn't have to remind him of that.

"I'll rearrange some things and see you over there," Jason said.

But when Rick pulled up in front of the O'Brian house, there sat Linda Starr's Smart Micro Compact, and nothing else.

Taking a deep breath, steeling himself against his own weaknesses, Rick picked up the portfolio of information he had put together for her and went up those wide front stairs.

He had the unsettling feeling he was a man moving toward his own future.

Linda walked through the empty O'Brian house. Yesterday, it had seemed lovely and full of promise. Today, notepad in hand, it seemed as if she had bitten off more than she could chew. And she wasn't talking chocolate chip cookies, though she'd definitely bitten off a little more than she could chew there, too.

A blush rose in her cheeks at the thought.

She and Rick Chase had kissed.

Oh, there really hadn't been anything passionate about it. An almost platonic touching of lips. A brush more than a kiss. Yet in that brush, the tenderness of his lips against the softness of her own, something within her had taken wing.

Had it been hope? Hope that there could be a decent man out there? Hope that she might be able to trust again?

But he had lied about his reasons for coming to her. That hardly seemed like a good basis for a trusting relationship!

"I am not beginning a relationship," she told herself firmly. Her voice echoed through the empty house.

Besides, he hadn't exactly *lied.* He had just omitted the fact that Bobbi had encouraged his reappearance in her mother's life. It hadn't been *his* idea to come by, to involve Linda in the renovation of this house. She really should have been much more insulted!

"I should have smacked him," Linda decided. "Maybe I will next time I see him."

She had never been that kind of person, a person of great furies and great passions. On the other hand, she was still trying to find out who she really was. Maybe she was one of those women who could coldly slap a man across his face so hard it would turn his head.

Unfortunately the very thought made her giggle. She was thirty-eight years old, *giggling*.

She was a different person than she had been yester-day. Before that damned kiss had clouded everything, including how she *should* have been reacting to the fact that Rick had not come to her on his own accord.

"Concentrate," she ordered herself, aware she had developed the habit of talking out loud. Unfortunately that probably said more about who she really was than slapping someone! Eccentric and solitary, becoming set in her ways. No wonder she had gotten on with Mildred Housewell!

Notepad in hand, Linda began in the basement and moved upward, increasingly aware of the enormity of this project. Electrical and heating had to be modernized. Insulation would need to be upgraded. Walls had to come out. Ceilings had to be replastered. New cabinets had to be installed. Windows had to be fixed or replaced. Hardwood had to be stripped, repaired, redone. A horrible add-on porch would need to be removed. Still, instead of feeling overwhelmed, as her list grew, Linda felt engrossed, captivated by the house and the bridge she was in charge of building between what it was and what it could be.

"Linda?"

She froze. Was she ready to see him again? Silly, to want to step into that empty closet, close the door and pretend she wasn't here. This timid reaction from the woman who had contemplated slapping him! But the truth was, she didn't feel anything like slapping him. She was wondering how to keep herself from staring at his lips!

"Up here," she called, straightening her skirt. She regretted the sensibility of the outfit—a gray straight line skirt, matching jacket, flat shoes. It was not the outfit of a kisser or a slapper, though maybe it would suit someone who hid in closets!

She listened to him coming up the stairs, two at a time. So much masculine energy.

Do not look at his lips, she commanded herself.

He came into the tiny back bedroom.

She looked right at his lips! They were full and sexy, and, if she recalled, had tasted of chocolate and enchantment.

"Good morning," she said crisply.

"Linda."

His voice was deep and sensual.

Stop it.

He was wearing a beautifully cut navy-blue suit with a fine pin stripe, white shirt, navy patterned tie. The sexy business man, illustrated, if it were not for that hair springing up at the back of his head.

"I forgot—"

"What would you think if—"

They spoke at the same time and then both laughed awkwardly. She looked at the toe of her very practical shoe and then looked up at him.

He was looking at her lips!

Right now, the furthest thing from her mind was slapping him. Even if he kissed her again!

"I forgot to leave this stuff with you," he said.

The *reason* he had forgotten was burning in his eyes. Really, it should be illegal for a man to have eyes that shade of green—as calm, as tempting as a cool forest pond on a hot summer day.

She took the folder from him, and their hands brushed. How could she possibly be so aware of him? This was *Rick*. Rick, who had changed everything when he had kissed her last night.

"Thanks," she said. Her voice sounded clipped, someone who was trying way too hard to sound like a complete professional. She rushed on. "I like this room. I like its potential."

"I like it too, but it's very small."

"That's why I thought we should knock out the wall between this room and the next one," she said, looking carefully at her notes.

"Absolutely. Look, I just dropped by because somehow I ended up taking all the contractor information with me."

Of course. That was all. He was all business. Nothing about that kiss was haunting him. She glanced up. Except that he seemed to still be looking at her lips.

He looked swiftly away, went over to the window. "Nice view," he said.

"That's what I thought, too. It faces the backyard, which is extraordinarily private given we are practically in the heart of the city. I was thinking this room would make a terrific bathroom. A bigger window, an extraordinary tub, French doors right here through to the master suite."

Sheesh. She did not even want to be thinking of master suites—and the kind of things that happened in master suites—with him in the same room. But think of it she did. She could see the room as if those doors already existed: a space richly romantic. Dark, wide-paneled hardwood floors, an area rug, a canopied bed, French doors through to the bathroom where a hot tub would be filled with perfumed water and floating candles…

Canopied beds were not on the house restoration list! Neither was perfumed water and candles!

"Bathrooms are a huge selling point in houses at the high end of the market, like this one," Rick said approvingly. "There's a picture in one of these brochures that captures the spirit of it."

He reached for the folder he had just given her and opened it. He shuffled through then found what he was looking for, and handed it to her. He came close so that they could study the picture together.

"Exactly," she breathed.

The bathroom in the picture was spalike in its elegance. The sensuality of her imagined master suite was nothing in comparison to the room in the picture— marble floors, muted lighting, gold faucets, beautiful double sinks, even a towel warmer. But it was the exquisite tub that was the focal point of the room. Claw-footed, it had been seriously updated; it was obviously made for two.

She felt nearly weak with longing. She wasn't leaning toward him! He wasn't leaning toward her!

"Rick? Are you here?"

They must have been leaning toward each other because they snapped apart!

"That's Jason. I wanted you to meet him. I think he's the best contractor in the business, and the sooner we can get started the better."

"Agreed," she said.

Jason bounded into the room. He was all blond curls, rippling muscles and youth.

"This is Linda Starr, our new project manager," Rick said.

"Wow. You didn't tell me the project manager was a girl," Jason said.

"A woman." Rick had sounded slightly terse about that correction. Linda shot him a look.

Jason turned out to be an outrageous extrovert as they toured the house, and she shared some of her preliminary ideas and notes with him. He was funny and charming and, underneath all that, Linda could see he really knew his way around old houses. She found herself doing that horrible thing daughters absolutely hate: wondering if he would like Bobbi. She asked him a few questions about himself that wouldn't be considered strictly professional. He seemed more than delighted to answer. When she asked him what he thought his future held, something quieted in all that energy. He told her he hoped it held a special girl, a family, a puppy.

Linda smiled at that. A puppy! The self-confident young contractor was just a big kid! Rick, however, was looking daggers at her. Was he interpreting her interest in Jason as flirtatious? For heaven's sake! She and Rick had exchanged the world's briefest kiss, not posted bans at the church! Surely he could see that she and Jason were teasing each other, both very aware it was a game going nowhere. She was probably at least a dozen years Jason's senior.

"Helloooo."

Rick closed his eyes and groaned. "An appearance by the house haunter." And then he took Linda's elbow firmly in his hand. "I think you and I should go look at the bed and bath showroom. There's a new place called Serenity that we've been using. You may not have seen it yet."

She was taken aback. She didn't realize she and Rick were going to be picking out fixtures together! Not the bathtub! Please, not the bathtub.

He led the way down the stairs. Mildred was standing at the bottom. She glared at him then smiled at Linda.

"We were just leaving," he said.

Jason followed them down and ushered them all out the door.

"I'll be back in—" Linda glanced at Rick.

"A week," he said deadpan.

"Why don't you give me your number and I'll call you?" Linda told Mildred sweetly, ignoring Rick's jibe. "And Jason, I can't wait to work with you. When did you say you could start?"

"How about first thing in the morning?"

"That would be wonderful."

Rick held open the door of his vehicle for her. There was something about the set of his shoulders that told her he was feeling tense.

"What is it about that poor old woman that gets under your skin?" she asked.

"Who? Oh, Mildred."

So, it wasn't the arrival of the old woman that had made him tense?

"She reminds me of my ex-wife," he said, finally.

Linda laughed, which earned her a very black look. "Kathy? Kathy was gorgeous. Mildred is ancient!"

He glared at her. "I don't usually talk about my ex-wife."

"Well, maybe you should!"

"What would that accomplish?"

"You might feel better."

"I didn't feel bad—until now!"

"If someone like Mildred can remind you of someone like Kathy, you're obviously feeling bad somewhere inside."

"I am not!"

"Fine."

Silence. His face was set in stone. He pulled over violently and without warning to the side of the road.

"I hate it that my marriage failed," he said. "Hate it. When I took those vows, I meant them. It was the worst failure of my life."

"I know," she said softly.

"You do?"

"I always knew you felt that way, as if it was your fault."

"It was. I should have been able to make it work."

"Kathy was gorgeous," she said carefully. "Rick, she was also self-centered and demanding and unreasonable."

He sighed like a man who had been keeping a secret to himself, and said, "She was so damned controlling, Linda. No matter what I did for her, it was never right or never enough."

He stared at her, and then he smiled, ever so slightly. "Just like Mildred Housewell."

She smiled, too. "I guess."

"Is that your gift, Linda?" he asked softly. "Do you lead people to emotional places where they feel like they could get blown to smithereens, and instead they walk out the other side feeling better than they did before?"

She felt suddenly awkward. "Don't be silly. I don't have any gifts."

"No? You can't enchant a man with chocolate chip cookies? Or the right word at the right time?"

"No!"

"How about a smile? Can you enchant men with your smile?"

"That's ridiculous."

"Really? Why don't you ask Jason if it's ridiculous?"

"Jason?"

"He seemed quite taken with you."

She actually laughed at that.

"And you put that charm to good use. He's starting tomorrow. I bet it would have been next month for me."

"I did not charm him."

"Look, I just want to say that you've been married for twenty years, Linda. You don't know the new rules, what these young guys are like."

She snickered. She couldn't help it. "Are you trying to protect me from the realities of a brand-new world, Rick?"

"Yes, I am," he said with such furious feeling that it sent a shiver up and down her spine.

"You don't have to."

"He was flirting with you. And you were encouraging him!" He mimicked her voice, *"And what do you think your future holds, Jason?"*

"Do you want to know the truth?"

"Of course!"

"I did think he was a very attractive young man."

"I knew it," he growled.

"And I wanted to know if he would be acceptable to introduce to Bobbi when she comes home at Thanksgiving. I don't know why. It's the kind of gesture she truly does not appreciate. Resents, even. However, if you had met her last beau, you would understand. Rick, he played bongo drums."

"You liked Jason for Bobbi?" His voice was incredulous.

"Rick! I'm not interested in a young guy like that. Are you crazy?"

He shook his head. "I guess maybe I am," he said, and then he smiled with sweet apology and pulled up in front of a building that looked like a Colonial Manor and had one brass plate in front of it. *Serenity.*

She took a deep breath. Why did she think just about the last thing she was going to feel while looking at bath fixtures with Rick Chase would be serenity? And how could she be dreading the experience and looking forward to it at the very same time?

CHAPTER FIVE

RICK CHASE rarely found himself in awkward positions. But that's exactly how he felt as he opened the door for her in front of Serenity, the most upscale bath supplier in Calgary.

Had he actually been a tiny bit jealous of her interactions with Jason? Of course not! He simply felt protective of her. There were things she needed to know, things she wouldn't know after being out of circulation for so long.

It was a brand-new world. Did she know what a booty call was? A cougar? Did she know about the dangers of meeting people over the Internet? Not that he would have known about those things himself if he hadn't caught a daytime television show one afternoon when he'd been feeling a little under the weather. He did not want to be the one explaining the realities of the modern world to Linda! That wasn't part of the agreement he'd made with Bobbi.

He'd succeeded in enticing Linda back into the world, but he hadn't thought through all the ramifications of that! How much of her back-to-the-world education was he now responsible for?

If he kept this up, he was going to put the controlling ways of his ex-wife to shame! Caring about someone wasn't about owning them or controlling them. It was about protecting them and thinking about their best interests. Where did a guy draw the lines?

Looking at bathtubs together did not seem like the best place to start!

Serenity was a gorgeous shop. Rick had always enjoyed the richness and the quality of what they offered, but today he was aware that everything in the store was designed to appeal to the sensuality of the human senses. From the lighting to the aromas to the exquisite one-of-a-kind fixtures, this was not a store for people who thought having a bath was a simple matter of getting clean.

"My God," Linda murmured, not at all unhappily. "It's absolutely romantic in here. This is exactly the ambience we want for that master suite bath, isn't it?"

We. Romance. Ambience. Rick could feel a little bead of sweat breaking out on his forehead.

"Oh, look, that's a beautiful claw-foot." She moved gracefully across the showroom floor to an elegant bath unit. Rick followed.

It certainly wasn't a traditional claw-foot tub, though it had the gorgeous curved lines of one. Instead of actual claw feet, it sat on a raised dark wood pedestal. A matching handrail, attached with brass fixtures, was installed outside the tub beneath the luxurious curved lip of the flawless porcelain. The faucets, on the side of the tub, instead of at the end, were old-fashioned, also brass.

"It really matches the character of the house, doesn't it?"

He had to admit it did.

"It says it's a two-person tub," she said doubtfully.

He felt his mouth going dry. Really! He didn't want to be thinking about two-person tubs with Linda in the near vicinity. Or ambience. Or romance.

"Don't they have air-conditioning in here?" he asked, and pulled the collar of his shirt away from his neck.

"It doesn't look like two people could possibly be comfortable in it."

Linda had always struck him as faintly, well, prim. But he remembered this about her from when they had worked together years ago. She had an intensity of focus that blocked out everything else. She was not thinking of two specific people in a tub, as in him and her, she was thinking of the mechanics of the damn thing.

She walked around the tub twice, her frown growing. He looked around the store frantically. Wasn't there a fan in here?

Then, without warning Linda slipped off her shoes and stepped into the tub. She sat down, then slid into a reclining position. Despite her hands caught firmly to the hem, her skirt hiked up slightly, revealing just a hint of thighs so shapely he thought he was probably going to spontaneously ignite.

She looked at him, innocent of what she was doing to him, her brow furrowed in concentration. She wriggled her toes and released the hem of her skirt. She flung wide her arms, trying to gauge the width. Apparently she failed.

"Get in," she said. It sounded faintly like an order.

"Excuse me?" His voice cracked, not that she appeared to notice. She was thankfully stretching her toes out as far as she could, not looking at him.

"I think its long enough," she decided. "I just don't know about the width. You're an average size guy. Get in the tub."

"Well—" he pointed out to her "—you're in the tub."

"I know that! I'm trying to see if two people could possibly fit comfortably in here."

He looked around furtively. He was not getting in that tub with Linda Starr!

She seemed oblivious to his reticence. "This tub could not possibly hold two full-size people!"

He was willing to take her word on that!

But, oh no, she had to test it! "Get in," she said again.

If he made too big a fuss about getting in, she'd guess that he could barely breathe, that his mind was going places it had absolutely no right to go. See? This was exactly why she needed him to help her navigate the complexities of single life. She couldn't be doing things like this! What if she'd brought Jason tub shopping with her instead of him? Asking a man to share a bathtub with you was something the male mind was going to wildly and hopefully misinterpret, no matter what the circumstances.

Linda was lying in that tub in a very decent gray suit, but with the skirt hitched up like that, Rick was not thinking schoolteacher thoughts. He noticed her hose-encased toes were adorable—tiny, painted like little pink gumdrops. Probably to match her damned devil pajamas!

His face felt as if it was on fire, as if he was a schoolboy who had come across that pretty school teacher lying in her tub in nothing but bubbles and floating flowers.

He glanced around again. The store was empty. Linda was going to guess his reluctance if he didn't do something quick!

Telling himself it was this kind of attention to detail that paid huge dividends in the housing market he served, Rick Chase hurriedly shook off his shoes and stepped over the side of the tub.

Now what?

Linda scooted over as far as she could and patted the place beside her. "Right here," she said. "Don't you think people want to take baths side by side if they're buying a two-person tub?"

"I have no idea," he muttered, amazed his voice worked at all. He actually closed his eyes before he turned around. He intended to ease into the spot beside her. Instead, his socks slid on the slippery surface and he went down hard.

"Ouch," she said.

"Sorry."

He tried to move, but he was wedged firmly in the tub beside her. She was going to feel the heat rolling off him in an uncomfortable wave.

"Just as I thought," she said, totally unaware of his heat. "Too small. Even though we are dressed and normally…"

She stopped, and he dared not look at her.

Her voice was strained, but trying valiantly for an all-business tone, she continued, "Okay, Rick, try it the other way, down at the other end."

Have mercy.

He tried, once more, to move. The tub was deeper than it first appeared and way too narrow. "I think I'm stuck," he whispered.

"You are not!" She managed to free one of her arms enough to push his shoulder. It seemed to wedge him in tighter. His sock clad feet were slippery on the polished bath surface, and he couldn't get the traction he needed.

She wriggled helpfully.

He did not feel in the least helped.

For a moment she was absolutely silent, contemplating their predicament. Then her laughter rang out, sweet and clear, and somehow it made the humiliation of his current position worth it. He became very aware of her thigh pressed into his, the softness of her shoulder, the smell of her hair.

"Roll over," he commanded, taking charge before this got totally out of hand. "We'll be skinnier sideways. One, two, three."

He rolled over onto his side. So did she.

He found the soft swell of her breast pressed against his chest. If it was at all possible they were more trapped than before.

Her eyes met his, and the merriment in them died, replaced with something hotter. She licked her lips, nervously, and yet the result was as sensual as a touch. He remembered, all too well, the taste of those lips. Now, with her body pressed against the length of his, everything else seemed to fade—the lights, the store, the sounds—everything except her.

She reached up with one hand, and he held his breath, thinking she was going to touch his cheek, or his brow, or maybe his lips. Instead she smoothed down that untamable spike of hair at the back of his head, the rooster tail that had tormented him—and his mother—since childhood. He started to breathe again.

"Oh," she said, and her eyes went very wide, just as if she had touched his cheek or his brow or his lips. She went very still as she apparently contemplated the fact that they were in a bathtub together, chest-to-chest, stuck. A blush, worth every ounce of his discomfort rose in her cheeks. She made a wild scramble to get out of the tub, but instead only managed to wedge herself more firmly against him.

"Get me out of here," she said.

"Okay, okay, don't panic."

"I am not panicking!" she retorted, but he could feel the flutter of her heart against his.

Then a salesman was peering over the side of the tub at them, his expression astounded. "May I help you?" he asked uncertainly.

"A can opener might be nice," Rick said.

"This is not a two-person tub," Linda informed the man, mustering her dignity despite the roses staining her cheeks. "It's advertised as a two-person tub."

"Perhaps it's manufactured in a country where

people are somewhat smaller," the salesman offered tactfully. "Or where they bathe with their clothes—"

Rick shot him a warning look and he shut his mouth with a snap.

With all the dignity of a celebrity leaving her limo, Linda managed to get a hand free. She offered it to the salesman. He took it and tugged. Nothing happened. He tugged a little harder and with a tiny popping sound, Linda broke free and scrambled to her feet.

Even though he was in a position to look right up her skirt, Rick did the gentlemanly thing. He closed his eyes as she stepped over the lip of that tub. Then he took the hand proffered to him and was also free.

"Newlyweds?" the salesman asked.

Linda's blush deepened to scarlet, and she concentrated on fixing her skirt, which was bound slightly and showing off legs that were absolutely glorious.

Rick noticed the salesman watching avidly and gave the man a killer look.

"Business partners," he said, taking a card from his pocket and giving it to the salesman, a diversionary tactic to keep the man's eyes off Linda's rather delectable derriere while she adjusted her skirt and put her shoes back on.

The salesman looked at the card, and Rick saw respect in his expression as he registered the name.

"Mercer Mainland," he introduced himself, and then added, "this model does come in a larger size."

"How much larger?" Linda asked. "Wider?"

"I'll just go get the specs," Mercer said and hurried off.

While he was gone, Rick put on his shoes. Linda wandered into other show bathrooms. He kept his distance a few paces behind her just in case she got it into her head to test drive another of the tubs.

"Too modern," she said of one particularly large jetted tub. "It doesn't go with the atmosphere."

Rick thanked the gods that she didn't get in that one, though it was more than evident that it would hold two people. Maybe more. That was the kind of world it was now, the kind of world Linda was naively unaware of. What if she innocently got involved with the kind of people who had tub parties for a crowd?

Thankfully Mercer came back with the new specs and pictures of the larger product before Rick had to think about how to protect her from tub parties. The danger to Linda was much more imminent. Mercer was none too subtly smitten.

Rick hoped she was aware of it. Maybe that was why she selected the rest of the fixtures—the fountain sink, glass shower enclosure, toilet, towel warmer—rapidly. Rick told the man to put it on the Star Chaser account, but Mercer still found a way to hand Linda his business card.

"Isn't that sweet?" Linda said, on her way out to the vehicle, arms laden with complimentary white bath towels.

Rick tried to recall if he'd ever received even one complimentary towel. He was pretty sure he had not.

"He put his home phone number on the back in case I need to reach him after hours!"

"Sweet," Rick said, his lips so tight they hurt. *Sweet?*

Which meant despite his hopes, she had not picked up on the fact that Mercer was practically inviting her to check out bathtubs with him. He glanced at her. She really didn't have a clue. Okay. So, the education of Linda Starr was going to be up to him.

Where did a man start once he had accepted responsibility for such a complex task? Obviously he couldn't lecture her. He had to slip her little bits of the wisdom he'd learned over several years of life as a single man and from his education thanks to daytime TV. He would have to be the very epitome of delicacy and subtlety. He had to let her know how men *really* thought. What it really meant when the bathtub salesman put his home number on the back of his business card.

He groaned.

"Are you all right?"

"Fine."

"I wouldn't mind looking at some flooring options, but I can do that by myself. Just drop me back at the house and I'll pick up my car."

Do it by herself? Oh, sure. Who knew what tests she thought the master bedroom flooring should be able to pass? Who was she going to encounter at the flooring store? There were versions of Jason and Mercer on every corner! And Rick hadn't had time to educate her about what they really wanted. They wanted to taste her lips and share her bathtub.

Just like he did.

Just like he had!

He was being faintly ridiculous, and he knew it. He also knew, from a quick glance at his watch, that he'd already missed two appointments this morning. Rick Chase did not miss appointments! His life was unraveling. He needed to look at that as a sign. To back off. To regain some of his customary control and composure. To reevaluate what was going on, and what he wanted to be going on.

Instead he heard himself saying, "I'll come look at flooring. I don't have a lot scheduled today."

"Great," she said.

He'd been absolutely right to accompany her. She was enchanted by his friend that restored old barn wood, and the feeling was obviously mutual. Did she think Ed wasn't still a man just because he was seventy-two?

At the end of the day Rick was utterly exhausted. Linda looked gorgeous and energized, her eyes sparkling with life as she chattered happily about *her* tub and the flooring choices.

He dropped her off at her car.

"Thanks, Rick, what a wonderful day!"

And it had been wonderful. Exhausting and wonderful. He had so much to teach her it made him even more exhausted just thinking about it.

"What would you say to a spin with me on my motorcycle on Saturday?" he asked casually. It would be perfect. They could stop for coffee and sightseeing, and he could educate her about all the sordid traps men laid for women like her.

She went very still. She looked at him so long, he

thought he would fall into her eyes and never come back out.

Then the loveliest smile tickled her lips. Gentle, a little bit scared.

That smile confirmed the wisdom of what he was doing. It was exactly why she needed him to show her the ropes. She was newly released into the world and she was scared. Well she should be. The woods were full of wolves. And snakes.

"I'd love that," she said. "What do I wear to ride a motorcycle?"

Suddenly he had the awful, awful feeling that Linda-in-black-leather was going to be worse than Linda-in-the-bathtub.

The things a man did in the name of duty!

"I'll dig up something for you," he promised.

Linda checked the address one more time, parked her car in the driveway and got out. Rick's condo complex, row style rather than the more typical apartment style, looked tasteful and expensive. The exterior was red brick with large front windows shuttered in white. The walkway lead up to the carved wooden door. The condo looked solid and masculine, a perfect match for a man like Rick.

She had not seen him since they had shopped for the bathtubs and flooring together a few days ago. But she talked to him on the phone, sometimes more than once a day, checking details, seeking advice, learning from his experience, coming to rely on his expertise.

She fell a little more in love with the O'Brian house every day even though it was as cranky and difficult as an old woman. She loved the work. She loved getting up in the morning and having a place to go, something to do. Not just something, but a job that she loved. She wondered what had taken her so long to get back into the swing of life, and even felt reluctantly grateful to her daughter for setting the wheels in motion. And today, to go along with her rediscovered passion for old houses, the new and improved Linda Starr was having her very first ride on a motorcycle.

Rick must have been waiting for her, because he opened the door as she came up the walk. He was dressed in a white T-shirt and jeans with black leather chaps strapped over top of them. The outfit hinted at a renegade inside the successful businessman and the chaps made his legs look long and strong and sexy. The rooster tail even looked as though it belonged to *this* Rick, and she remembered suddenly, how it had felt underneath her fingertips, soft and springy.

She stopped and regarded him, remembered other things. The taste of his lips on hers, the hardness of his body pressed against the length of hers in that bathtub.

"This isn't a date is it?" she blurted out.

He threw back his head and laughed.

"Not if that would make you feel awkward. Besides—" he lowered his voice and leaned toward her "—once you've shared a bathtub with a guy the awkward stage is over. You want to see the place, or do you want to go?"

Of course she had that purely feminine desire to see

his place and to see what secrets it would reveal. His home was tidy and tasteful, the decor sophisticated. The only secret she learned was one she had already guessed: Rick Chase belonged to a much larger world than she did.

"While I was spending my days wiping noses as the classroom helper and devoting my life to keeping the tablecloths snowy-white, you were seeing Africa," she said, feeling inadequate, touching the hand-carved wooden giraffe that fit so perfectly with the leather in his living room.

He touched her arm. "Linda, don't say that as if one choice was better than the other. They were just different. That's all. Don't you know how I would look at you sometimes, and wish things could have worked out differently for me?"

She snorted. "Like when?"

"Like that Christmas after my divorce when you invited me over so much. Don't you know how I yearned to be the one putting the little homemade ornaments on the tree? Trying to figure out how to assemble the tricycle?"

"Are you serious?"

"Oh, yeah."

She looked into his eyes and knew he meant it. Her husband had had it and had never once shown a single iota of appreciation. Marriage, family obligations—those were Blair's prison. Today was not a time to think of things like that. It was a time to embrace this brand-new adventure her life had become.

"Here. I found you some leathers. You can change in the downstairs bathroom—no tub you might be tempted to try—and we'll be on our way."

She had to slug him in the shoulder for that. He grinned, and the differences between their worlds and their choices slipped away.

If she had been hoping she might appear sexy in black leather, she was gravely disappointed.

The outfit was slightly too large for her. Still, it was obviously made for a woman. Had he ridden with women before? Of course he had. And probably did. His life was none of her business. Maybe she should have asked herself these questions before she came here. Where was it going? What were his intentions? What were hers?

But looking at herself in the mirror, she realized she was being far too serious. Couldn't she just have fun? Did she always have to analyze everything? Look for the possibility of a broken heart way up the road?

Would Rick break her heart?

"We aren't anywhere near there," she told herself sternly. "We are two old, old friends who are going to spend the day together."

But that wasn't what registered in his eyes when she emerged from the bathroom.

"You look very beautiful," he said.

She scowled at him. That was no way to start a day of two old friends spending some time together.

"Hey! What are you looking at me like that for?"

"I don't want things to become complicated between us," she said softly.

"Okay," he said, his voice deliberately light. "No bathtubs, no cookies, no kisses."

"Perfect," she said with determination, but that's not how she felt when he helped her put on the helmet and then put on his own. They went through an adjoining door to his garage, and, moments later, she was sitting astride a motorcycle for the first time in her life, clinging to him with all her might. No complications? This experience was at least as sensual as sharing a tub! Despite the faint barrier of black leather, Linda could feel his every move, the strength of his body, his every muscle, where her own body fitted into the curves of his.

Linda had thought she might be afraid, and she did feel very vulnerable on the back of the bike. But she soon saw that he handled the machine with confidence, sliding in and out of traffic with ease. In the strangest and most delightful way, riding the motorcycle behind him was like dancing with him, gauging his moves, leaning with him, shifting her weight, anticipating. The purr of the powerful engine vibrated up through her body, making her tingle with the most wonderful awareness.

Soon they were out of the city, on the open road. Conversation was impossible, yet she could not help but feel they were communicating at a level that was without words. He leaned. She leaned. She could read how relaxed he was because of how closely she was pressed into him.

She could also tell that he was in good shape. Being this close, physically, to a man made her realize she was hungry for touch. Under normal circumstances, she might have fought that hunger, but on a motorcycle it was the most natural thing in the world to give herself over to the pure enjoyment of the play of his muscles beneath her hands.

The day was warm, a perfect late summer day—the beginning of rich golds in the leaves, the sun gentle on the flat grassland that surrounded the highway.

He turned at the hamlet of Claresholm and took a secondary road that snaked them through craggy coulees and foothills, past ranches. They saw a group of cowboys herding cattle from horseback, and began to catch glimpses of the Rocky Mountains in the distance.

He pulled over to the side of the road and cut the engine. "Look."

He was pointing at a huge bird that she recognized from her newly acquired bird books. It was a golden eagle, larger even than the bald eagle. It sat on the very top of a huge tree glaring down at them. It spread its wings and flew. They watched, silent and awed, and then he turned to her.

"How are you doing?"

"Loving it," she admitted. "It feels so free. Probably as close to flying as what people ever get to feel."

He nodded. "The bonus—you don't have to be anywhere near a parachute."

They watched the bird for a while longer and then re-straddled the bike. Soon they came to a different highway, and he turned back the way they had come, making the ranch lands loop. Now they were in truly spectacular country, wooded copses, spruce-capped foothills rolling toward the majesty of the white-capped rugged Rockies to the west. The road dipped and twisted and turned, trees gave way to the grasslands of Alberta's famous range country. Now, the road had long straight stretches that climbed out of coulees, up to spectacular ridges, and then down into riverbeds. They went past ranches with big wooden post gates and storybook names and herds of fat cattle. They saw—and smelled—pump jacks dotting the landscape. They looked like the perpetual motion ducks that could be purchased at any novelty store, but these ducks pulled oil from the ground. Finally they came to a tiny town, Longview, and Rick stopped his motorcycle in front of the singer Ian Tyson's coffee shop, the Navajo Mug.

They ordered coffee and, with a wicked grin, Rick also grabbed two of the oversize chocolate chip cookies for sale.

"You promised no cookies," she reminded him, but bit into hers with delight anyway. They looked at the Western art displays, gifts and paintings and then sank onto an inviting leather sofa.

"So," he said, "I have an ulterior motive for today."

She hoped it was the same as hers, though hers seemed to have changed ever so subtly since this morning when she'd been determined not to have any complications! She looked at his lips and then looked away swiftly to a window facing the grass, the hills, the cattle, the pump-jacks.

"I want to find out what you know about being single in this day and age."

"Give me an example of what you mean," she suggested. He was looking adorably uncomfortable.

"Well," he said, his discomfort increasing, though his tone was extra casual. "For example, do you know, er, what a booty call is?"

Unfortunately she had just taken a rather large bite of her cookie. Now, it went down the wrong way, and she began to choke. Rick pounded on her back. The waitress even came over looking worried. She was going to die laughing! What a delicious way to go! But her windpipe cleared, and she took the water glass Rick offered her, sipped a bit and met his eyes.

"Rick! I have an eighteen-year-old daughter. Of course I know what that is. The question is, how do you?"

He looked disgruntled. "Oprah," he confessed.

She laughed again, and loved the way the laughter felt. When had all the fun drained so completely out of her life? Unfortunately she knew the exact day, but she wasn't going to go there. Not today, not when she was with this delightful man, who she suspected had the misguided idea he needed to protect her from a world gone wild.

Just as if she did not suspect his motive, Linda covered Rick's hand with hers. "What kind of question was that, anyway?"

"It was just a question," he said defensively. "Conversational."

"No, it wasn't."

He sighed. "Okay, I was worried about you. You know, reentering the world. Young guys finding you attractive. You might get, well, hurt."

"Young guys finding me attractive?" she echoed, astounded.

"Like Jason!"

"Jason calls me Mom," she told Rick, almost gently.

"He does?"

"I brought him a homemade sandwich last week and made lemonade for him, and that was that."

"Well, I wasn't talking about Jason, specifically, anyway. Just about guys in general. I think you should know what to expect."

She was glad she was not eating more cookie. She thought she would probably choke again she was trying so hard not to laugh. "What a good idea," she said sweetly. "Why don't you tell me everything you know?"

CHAPTER SIX

IN THE gathering darkness, Rick watched Linda's little car do an effortless U-turn in front of his home. She gave him a jaunty wave and drove away.

That, he thought, *did not go particularly well.* His goal in spending the day with Linda had been to educate her, to help her get ready for the world she was reentering, a world full of lecherous men who would lie to her and take advantage of her. She was an extremely well off woman and an extremely attractive one. That could make her a target for the unscrupulous and the players. Instead he had gotten lost somewhere along the way, his plan forgotten, put aside, lost in her laughter, the feeling of her arms wrapped so tightly around his waist, her leather-encased curves pressed against his back, her legs touching his legs… How was a man supposed to remember what he had set out to do, what he was *supposed* to do, in circumstances like that?

He'd probably made a complete fool of himself, but at least he'd found out she knew what a booty call was. Her eyes had widened to the size of the silver dollars that decorated the saddle beside their couch in the Navajo Mug when he had explained a cougar.

"So," she'd said, "it's an older woman who finds younger men attractive?"

"I think, er, more precisely, its an older woman who *hunts* younger men."

"Hunts," she had repeated, mulling it over, taking a sip of her coffee and then looking directly into his eyes. Were hers still sparking with a hint of laughter? "But the prey are willing?"

Oh, yeah. Did she not know anything about men? "Yes."

"Oh. So do you think I might be like that?"

He glared at the innocent expression on her face before he realized she was being deliberately obtuse. She had probably known what a cougar was all along!

"No, I do not think you are like that! But I wanted you to know, because a younger man, say like Jason, might mistakenly *think* you were like that."

Well, maybe not Jason. Rick had been relieved to hear the young contractor was calling Linda *Mom.*

"It all seems very complicated," she'd said with a sigh.

"Do you watch daytime television?" he asked. She'd been at home for twenty years, she was probably way more well versed in this stuff than he was.

"No," she said. "When I have a spare moment, I prefer to read."

Which, he realized, dismally, still left the educating thing up to him.

Now, he was waving goodbye to her, aware that he

had mostly failed in his mission. He'd warned her about booty calls and the possibility of being mistaken for something she was not, but then he'd been lured away from his purpose. Sitting there in the Navajo Mug, he'd given himself over to the simple pleasure of being with her. And it was a pleasure. She was a woman of his age, his generation. They understood the same issues, they had common ground. They talked of old houses and new ones. Conversation was easy between them, and laughter lurked at the edges of everything. He did not know his life had become so serious until she made the laughter come back.

After coffee, which had lasted late into the afternoon, they had toured the art and antique shops in the small ranch towns on that route—Longview, Black Diamond, Turner Valley, Bragg Creek. He had not really expected that darkness would be falling by the time he pulled back into his own driveway, but it had been.

And still, he'd been strangely reluctant to end the day.

It had been Linda who had insisted she needed to go home.

"Rick, I'm still living out of boxes! I have to unpack."

Now, watching her drive away, he recalled he had promised he would help her unpack. Should he go over there?

No!

That wasn't the plan. From the very first moment that Bobbi had enlisted his aid, Rick had known he was going to need a plan to help Linda effectively. Today was ample proof of that. He'd gotten seriously off track.

He hadn't given her one tool today that might help her reenter the world. Unless laughter counted. And now, if some young guy came on to her too aggressively, she would know she'd been mistaken for a cougar.

Though only a blind person would ever look at her and see anything but what she was: softness, light and sincerity.

He remembered that kiss, and how it had scorched his soul. His mind went directly to Linda in a bathtub-built-for-two. So, then again maybe not *all* softness, light and sincerity. If he could barely control his thoughts—he who very nobly only had her best interests at heart—how could he possibly trust her to the general male population, swines one and all? That's why he had to stay on track. He could not go over there and help her unpack boxes. Things between them might go to the very place he wanted to warn her about.

With every ounce of his discipline he marched into the house and turned on his computer. He made a careful list of what Linda needed to guard against and look for in a man: She needed to know if he was employed, and for how long, and if he made good money; she needed to know about his past relationships and how he got along with his family; she needed to know about his loyalty, his ability to commit, how trustworthy he was, if he used substances, how involved he was in his community.

Rick couldn't let her jump back into dating without arming her with the information she needed. She liked to read, so he used the Internet to find books for her. There was quite a selection: how to find the perfect mate, how to decipher the language of the wily male animal. Rick was exhausted by the time his homework was done. He had placed orders for half a dozen of the more promising books.

If he was honest, he was just a little bit heart sore. He didn't want to think about Linda leading the kind of life these books were designed to help with. It was a jungle out there. She was going to get hurt.

He looked at his list again, studied it hard.

One thing became perfectly clear: the perfect man for Linda was him.

Except for one thing. He had yet to be completely honest with her. And because he had given his word to a dead man, he never could be.

He contemplated Blair's final secret, felt the weight of it. There was a child out there. She would be two years old very soon. Her aunt Tracy, Blair's mistress's sister, young and scared, had risen to the challenge of being a mother to Blair's orphaned daughter.

Rick administered the trust fund and fielded the frightened phone calls of a young woman barely out of her teens.

Blair's secret. And his.

Rick sighed and cradled his head in his hands, suddenly feeling unbearably weary. Why even think of telling Linda? Hadn't she suffered enough at Blair's hands? What would knowledge of Blair's final treachery accomplish?

Still, that secret, and his role as keeper of it, meant that he was not the perfect man for her. He was both sad and relieved by that knowledge.

He forced himself to look back at the list he had made, forced himself to think analytically, to try and be practical about this. He should help her find the right man. He should, at the very least, help her develop the criteria for finding the right man. But he could not be that man. Because she would never forgive him for this thing he was keeping from her. That's why enjoying her company today had been so, so wrong. Because he knew something that she didn't: It could never be.

Still, he was as responsible for her as he was for Blair's secret. He picked up the phone and dialed.

"Oh, hi." She sounded surprised to hear from him. And happy.

"How about dinner tomorrow night?" he asked.

"Sure." She sounded surprised and happy again.

Armed with the books, gift wrapped just for her, he sat at dinner with her the next night. Somehow the perfect moment to take them out of the back of his vehicle and give them to her never arrived. So, he dropped by the O'Brian house the next day. There she was covered in plaster dust, her hair white with it.

It was an astonishing preview of what she would look like in thirty years. She was going to be just as gorgeous, silver-haired, as she was now. He ended up going over some things about the house with her, rather than giving her the books.

Under Linda's hand, the house was becoming so much more than a house. Her touch with color and detail were transformative. Even Mildred, who was there to help pick ceramic tile for the kitchen, smiled at him.

He took them both out for lunch.

He swore he would give her the instruction manuals on man-hunting the very next time he saw her. But then he was invited to an open house. Who would love that more than Linda?

He picked her up at the O'Brian house and they walked through the tree-lined, curving streets of the beautiful old neighborhood. Leaves were taking on hues of gold and red, and they crunched beneath their feet.

There was wine and cheese at the open house, which was for sale by a friendly competitor. Rick and Linda walked around looking at the details, getting ideas, making comparisons. He introduced her to his competitor, Ray Jurrassi, a man he liked and respected very much.

Ray called him that night.

"Is there something between you and the lady you brought to the open house? Did you say she's your project manager?"

"And Blair's widow."

"Ah." Loaded with knowing. Everyone had known about Blair.

"Look, if I'm not stepping on your toes, would you mind if I called her?"

"What? As a project manager?"

Ray laughed, a little uncomfortably. "No. Something a little more personal than that."

Rick was silent. Wasn't this everything he'd asked for for Linda? A man who was respectable and employed and successful? A man who was, as far as he knew, totally honorable? Ray was a widower, not divorced. He was devoted to his adult children and coached his grandson's baseball team.

"She's not ready," Rick heard himself saying, but he knew it was a different truth he was discovering.

He was not ready. He did not want to see Linda going out with another man, and it wasn't because he was failing so miserably in educating her, either. He hung up the phone and tried to decide what that meant.

He had a sudden inspiration. He wasn't going to give Linda those books. And he certainly wasn't going to introduce her to any hopefuls like Ray. No more thinly disguised lectures on the dangers of the world. Linda couldn't possibly find the perfect man, or even a worthy one, because he knew, as an expert on the subject, that there was no such thing.

The answer was so obvious! Her happiness did not lie in finding a man. That was an old-fashioned notion, and he should be ashamed he had ever entertained it. Her answer was in finding purpose, like in the O'Brian place.

Now, he just had to find a hobby for her to fill up her evening hours. He thought hard about what he had learned about her. She liked bird-watching. She liked old things. She liked cooking. Night class! That was it. He'd talk her into night class.

But what was he thinking? It was probably the equivalent of the lonely heart's club for the over thirty set, which brought him back to square one. Some great books she could study at home, maybe some videos.

He was back on the Internet, fingers flying as he placed orders for Linda. *Bird-watching for Beginners; Refinishing Fine Furniture; More Dough Than You Know What to Do With, A Guide to Making Bread.* He chuckled happily to himself as he filled his virtual shopping cart.

Then he stopped.

For some reason, he thought of the expression on her face when she had asked Jason to tell her what he'd wanted from life. When Jason had said a puppy, she had nearly melted.

He sighed with relief. A ton of books and a dog for Linda. Her life would be full! And what more perfect companion than a canine? Loyal. A good listener. Affectionate. It could even provide her with a sense of security in that less than stellar neighborhood she had chosen for herself.

Whistling the happy whistle of a man *finally* on the right course, Rick took the gift-wrapped books on dating, mating and everything in between from his briefcase, hesitated, and then threw them all, still wrapped, in the garbage.

Now, all that was left to do was to find just the right dog…

Linda sat in her spare room, surrounded by towering boxes. She tugged one down from the stack and opened it without any real interest. Tupperware. She closed the box and wrote Storage on it. She opened the next one. Towels. Enough towels for a manor house with four bathrooms. Towels that Blair had used.

She closed that box, too, and wrote Charity.

She didn't want to be thinking of Blair right now, hated it that he had crept sneakily into her thoughts just when she felt so wonderful about life.

She left the boxes and went to the bathroom. She liked what she saw in the mirror. Her hair was spiky and her cheeks were rouged by sun and wind and laughter. Her eyes were the eyes of a person who had decided to live. And to trust.

She thought of Rick handing out his not-so-subtle advice and smiled. What a dear friend. Was it ever going to be more? She had enjoyed the past week more than she had the right to enjoy anything. Every time he showed up unexpectedly, her heart turned over. Every time her phone rang she hoped, a little guiltily, that it was him.

Rick made her laugh, and he made her think. In some ways he was as comfy as a favored old leather chair and in other ways it was exciting to be with him—a whole world unexplored that whispered across his lips and danced through the green of his eyes.

"Don't get ahead of yourself, sweetie," she said. "Just play it day by day."

That was what grief had taught her, grief made worse in that death was intertwined with betrayal. Blair had died in a hotel fire. In the company of the mistress Linda had known nothing about. Her husband had been making a fool out of her for years, and she had been blissfully engrossed in running her household, raising her daughter.

Or maybe blissful was too strong a word. Even though

her life had filled her with satisfaction, she'd known things were wrong between she and Blair. He'd married her because he had to. The marriage—the baby—had been Linda's reason for being and his life sentence. So, she had been in the dreadful position of trying to make it up to him, trying desperately to be anything he wanted her to be, so he wouldn't resent her and Bobbi.

Linda took a deep breath, cherishing her freedom from all that *trying,* all that tension.

Now she allowed herself to feel furious with him. How dare he make her feel like that? How dare he see Bobbi—beautiful, precious Bobbi—as a trap rather than a miracle? How dare he treat the suggestion they have more children with contempt? How dare he treat Linda's love as if it was *owed* to him, as if it was nothing more than a rug at the door that he could wipe his feet on?

The next box she opened was crystal: a carefully packed and priceless serving bowl, a wine decanter, champagne flutes. Blair had loved every symbol of wealth. For birthdays and anniversaries and Christmases he had given her crystal, added to *his* collection, oblivious to the fact that all she wanted was one gift, just one, that said he knew her.

Linda closed the box, but she didn't label this one. She took it down to her cellar. The room was concrete, empty and grim. It held a furnace and four walls.

She opened the box and picked up the bowl. She hurled it with all her might at the cement wall, and it exploded. By the time she'd emptied that box, a pile of shattered glass was heaped at the bottom of the cement

wall and she had screamed herself hoarse. She had
called Blair every word she had not allowed herself to
say for more than twenty years. She had cursed him and
hurled her fury at him against that wall. She had ignored
the tears that streamed down her face. Now her fury was
spent. She sank to the floor and shook with exhaustion
and spent emotion. She looked at the pile of broken
glass and a giggle escaped her.

Linda Starr, alone in her basement, shrieking like a
fish wife, screaming out words that would have made a
sailor blush! She giggled again at how ludicrous a
picture she must make. Then she began to laugh. She
laughed like a woman who had been set free. She
laughed until her stomach hurt. She laughed with joy
and freedom and hope and discovery. That place in her
that turned hard and cold every time she thought of
Blair seemed blessedly empty of venom.

She took the empty box upstairs and shut the door
on the basement. She would clean it up a different day.
Tonight she just wanted to enjoy this feeling—of being
ready for the next wonderful thing in her life.

The phone rang and she saw it was Bobbi.

"You'll never guess what I've been up to!" she told her
daughter. She gave Bobbi all the details of the motorcycle ride: the eagle, the coffee at the Navajo Mug, the visits
to the antique stores. She told Bobbi how the O'Brian
house was progressing, told her about Mildred and Jason.

She left out the perfect ending, which was lying shattered in her basement.

"Mom?" Bobbi said.

Linda's heart went still. She had been talking so much about herself! She'd been completely insensitive. Now she realized her daughter was crying!

"What's wrong?"

"Wrong?" Bobbi breathed. "Mom, nothing's wrong. I've never heard you sound so happy. It makes me happy."

"You mean you've never heard me sound so happy since your dad died," Linda clarified uncertainly.

"No, I don't mean that. I mean I've never heard you sound so happy, ever."

All those years of coming up with the perfect theme for the birthday party, sewing the costumes for the school play, decorating the house like a fairy tale for Christmas, and she had never fooled anyone, Linda thought, except herself.

They spoke a while longer. When Linda hung up the phone she stood at the window that overlooked the darkness of the backyard. Now she understood her fascination with that whooping crane. He represented what she'd never had. Freedom. The opportunity at last to be happy.

It was the first time in many years that she was responsible only for herself. She could break dishes if she wanted to. Lay in her grass at dawn. Buy whatever kind of car she preferred, have long, hot bubble baths. Linda hugged herself, looked at the stars and made a wish: that she would finally know what it would be like to reach for one of them, to chase the stars. Happiness unfurled within her, a flag getting a breath of wind.

* * *

The next morning, Linda was underneath one of the additions on the O'Brian house with Jason. He was pulling wood away from the joists in great fistfuls. Unidentified particles were falling in her eyes, but that feeling of happiness remained.

"I think we should just pull it down," he said.

"I agree."

She inched her way out from under the house and was standing there brushing the cobwebs out of her hair when Rick pulled up. She shimmied out of her coveralls as if they were on fire. Jason slid out from under the house and gave her an appreciative look.

Remembering Rick's lecture on cougars she burst out laughing. "What are you doing over Thanksgiving, Jason?"

His jaw dropped. "I-I-I'm not s-s-sure."

"My daughter will be home from college. Maybe you'd like to drop by for dinner one night."

"Your daughter?" He looked concerned, a young man that didn't want to be entrusted with anyone's daughter. Especially not sight unseen! He scurried toward the house, some sudden and urgent business to attend to.

"Where's he rushing off to?" Rick asked.

Was he looking at poor Jason darkly?

"I offered to introduce him to Bobbi. I don't think he was wild about the idea."

"I guess not! The only time a mother sets up her daughter is if she has intentions. And if the daughter has something wrong with her. Two-headed. Four hundred pounds. That sort of thing."

"I don't have intentions. And of course you know there's nothing wrong with Bobbi."

"Yeah. I know. I don't want him to know."

"What have you got against Jason, anyway?"

"Nothing. Except he's a man. And I know exactly how men think. He doesn't want to date your daughter because he'd have to be decent to her, because he knows you."

"Rick! Are you cynical?"

His face said it all. But then, of course, he'd been friends with Blair for a long, long time. Perhaps that was where his cynicism stemmed from.

"I have something I want to show you," he said. "Come down to my car."

She walked with him, expecting another one of those great catalogs for houses. Instead he opened the back door and reached into a basket. A tiny ball of black blinked sleepily at her.

"Ohmygod," she breathed. "A puppy!"

Rick was beaming at her, the puppy nestled against the solidness of his chest. She took in the tender picture they made.

"Let me hold him," she said.

Rick surrendered him readily.

"He's beautiful," she whispered. The puppy whined a little bit and nestled into her.

"He is, isn't he?" Rick said with satisfaction.

"I've always been able to picture you with a dog, Rick."

"You can picture me with a dog?" His satisfied expression had been replaced with a slight frown, as if there was something not very masculine about picturing him with a puppy.

She said soothingly, "I think it's adorable. I was becoming concerned you were a man afraid of commitment. And a dog is a huge commitment."

"Adorable. Huge commitment," he muttered.

From the look on his face, she was talking him right out of his puppy!

"He's obviously a man's dog," she said reassuringly. "I mean look at the size of his feet! He's going to be a giant. I'm sure it will take a strong, strong person, just like you, to control him."

Rick did not look soothed by her flattery of his strength.

She held out a paw for Rick to inspect. "He looks like he's part lab." She laughed. "And part Newfoundland. Where on earth did you get him?"

"The shelter. He actually wasn't what I had in mind, but when he looked at me with those big, brown eyes, I thought he was the one."

She was sure she heard doubt again, so she rushed to convince Rick he'd made the right decision for himself.

She looked into those big, brown eyes herself. "You are going to have the most wonderful owner!" she told the puppy. "And I'll come visit you lots! Would that be okay, Rick?"

Was there the slightest hesitation before Rick said, "Well, actually, ah, yes, I guess so."

What was wrong with him?

"I may get a dog, too, someday," she said, thinking,

from the faintly bewildered look on Rick's face that he was second-guessing his decision. "But I was just thinking last night how wonderful it is to be responsible just for myself for a change."

"You were?"

"I was. Let's see if we can find a stick."

She put the puppy on the ground. He was really too young to be interested in sticks, but he gamboled around gamely in the leaves. At first, Rick held back, his hands in his pockets, looking faintly troubled, but naturally the puppy charmed him out of that in short order. Soon, they were chasing the dog and chasing each other, kicking up storms of leaves and laughing until it hurt.

Then she gave Rick, puppy tucked under his arm, a tour of the house. Even though he had seen it the day before, the changes in one day could be dramatic. Today new cupboards of maple and countertops of black marble were going in. The kitchen looked spectacular.

"Linda," Rick said, "you have done an extraordinary job. I don't know how I'm going to bear putting a For Sale sign on it."

She laughed, but felt the glow of his praise. "I'm feeling the same way. You know what I think I like the most?"

"What?"

"It gives me hope. Here is this old house, sagging, neglected, but all the elements of greatness were there, just waiting for some attention."

"And that gives you hope?"

"Yes," she said, "because I think people are like that, too."

"You are not suggesting you were sagging—" He actually blushed and then hurried on, "Or neglected."

"Oh, Rick, I was both. And I feel like what's happening to me is parallel to what's happening to this house. I'm getting a facelift."

"You are?"

"Rick," she pounded his arm. "My spirit is getting a facelift. I want to thank you for that. I know I would have found my way back to this world eventually, but I am so grateful for the push you gave me."

They were saved from an awkward moment by the dog dribbling on Rick's beautiful white shirt. In way of apology, he wriggled and licked Rick's face. Laughing like children they raced for the door.

"Thank you," she said quietly, "for restoring me." Then she stood on tiptoe, kissed him on the cheek and dashed inside the house before that awkward moment could reappear.

That night she dreamed about the puppy. In the dream, he had on a beautiful red bow, and Rick passed him to her, a gift.

When she woke, stunned, Linda went over their earlier encounter, word for word, remembering how Rick had seemed a bit bewildered, shocked even. She sat bolt upright in bed. Because he had intended to give the dog to her! He had never planned on being a pet owner! He had not bought that puppy for himself. He had bought it for her!

Suddenly—irrational or not—she had to know if that

was true, if Rick had bought the puppy for her or if her dreams were entangling themselves with reality. And she wanted to know in person. She glanced at her bedside clock. It was three-thirty in the morning. She was not one to make middle-of-the-night house calls.

On the other hand, she decided to experiment with being impulsive. She tossed a jacket and a pair of loose fitting jeans over her pajamas and hopped into her car. She was more than halfway to his house when she realized what she was doing was insane. What if she got pulled over? Little devils were peering out from under her jacket, and she was wearing house slippers!

Coming fully awake she realized she couldn't really confront Rick about the puppy when she didn't know how she felt about the gesture. Her initial reaction was one of tenderness. How cute that he would get her a puppy. But her second reaction was more complicated. She didn't really want a puppy. This stage of her life was for her. It would be easy to get distracted with what other people wanted for her. It would be easy to let that tenderness she felt for Rick cloud her judgment about what she wanted for herself.

Then, as she woke up even more, an even more startling realization hit her. This postmidnight trip to Rick's house wasn't about the puppy at all! It was to see if he was alone. It was suspicious residue left from her last life. How could a guy like that be by himself? He was probably just like Blair.

She didn't like thinking that way about Rick. She didn't like that leaden feeling in her heart. On the other hand, she had been fooled once before, terribly fooled. Scarred. Wasn't a little wariness at this stage of the game far more sensible than a whole lot of regret later?

"Well," she said out loud, aware that by talking out loud she was trying to convince herself to do something she was pretty sure was not right, "what would it hurt to drive by his place? If there's another car in the driveway then you know."

But the closer she got the more she became aware she didn't want to do this. She wanted to trust. Rick, yes, but herself more.

She wanted to know she was the kind of woman who could judge people accurately, who could trust her instincts. Besides, if she gave in to this temptation, what sneaky little thing would come next? Hang up phone calls in the middle of the night? Detective work around numbers on his cell phone?

"I will not be that kind of person," she decided.

But it was too late, because now she was on Rick's cul-de-sac, and there was no way out except to go up there, right by his place and turn around.

His house was dark. There was no other car in the driveway. And just as she allowed herself to feel the tiniest little shiver of relief, his front porch light came on and he stumbled out the door, in his housecoat, the puppy in his arms. He set the puppy on the ground and looked around sleepily.

Then he saw her. His eyes widened and he froze.

She wanted to shrink behind the steering wheel, to speed away, but it was too late. With a huge sigh, she realized she was going to have to pull over. No excuses, she was going to have to confess her crime. She *wanted* to confess her crime. Because she wanted what she had never, ever had. She wanted to be cared about, warts and all. She wanted to be cared about even if she harbored suspicions born of wounds that had nothing to do with him.

If she could trust her heart, it was telling her he might be the man to care about her, just the way she was.

CHAPTER SEVEN

AT FIRST, Rick thought he must be dreaming. He blinked hard and rubbed at his groggy eyes. There was no way Linda Starr was driving down his eerily quiet street at nearly four in the morning.

It was nothing more than a weird coincidence that a car identical to hers was the only thing, besides his energetically tree-sniffing puppy, moving in the silent cul-de-sac. He looked hard at the car to convince himself. It passed under the glare of a streetlight, illuminating a pale face. It was indeed her, wide-eyed and faintly sheepish.

She pulled over in his driveway and got out of the car. From the reluctance of her movements, Rick sensed guilt—a thief caught in the act—and got the definite sense she would much rather have not been seen.

But what could she possibly want from him at this hour?

"Hi," she whispered.

"Hi." If he was not mistaken, underneath the jacket she wore the pink fuzzy pajamas, the ones with devils cavorting on them. For the first time in his life he understood people really did pinch themselves to see if they were awake.

"What are you doing out here?" she asked casually, as if his presence in his own front yard, rather than hers, was the surprise.

"The dog book said it would be easier to house train Mr. Poo Jangles over there if I let him out a couple times during the night."

"That takes discipline," she said with approval.

It was a reminder that he had to be careful with Linda. A man could bask in her approval and completely forget to ask what the heck she was doing out at this time of night. On his street. At his house.

"The doggy-do book said pay now or pay later." See? Doggy-do, instead of *is there a reason for this nocturnal visit with your adorable PJ's poking out from under your jacket?* Speaking of the adorable pajamas, they were also peeking out from the waistband of jeans that were way too large for her. Whatever the reason, she had come here quickly.

"Is that what you're going to call him? Poo Jangles?"

And she wanted to make small talk. Rick felt inexplicably indulgent. It was surreal and kind of wonderful and crazy to be out on his front lawn, predawn, with a dog-in-potty-training and Linda-in-her-pajamas.

All this time, he'd traveled around the globe looking for new experiences and adventures, when the right person—or at least one person—could deliver a brand-new world right to his own yard. She was like a mysterious destination—it would take a man a lifetime to know her completely.

"Poo Jangles is about the nicest thing I've called him," Rick admitted, playing it her way and watching the dog. He couldn't help noticing his ill humor at having to come out at this hour seemed to have evaporated. "You don't even want to know what he got called at his midnight bathroom break."

"Actually I do."

A small thing, insignificant really, but it was spoken like a woman who wanted to know all about him, even in his less than sterling moments. So, he told her the horrible name he'd called the dog, and she pretended to be shocked and then laughed.

Well, if it was confession time, he might as well come all the way clean. "The old lady next door glared at me, even though I did pick it up from her grass."

Linda sighed. "You have no gift at all with old ladies."

"True." Was she insinuating he had some kind of gift with younger ones? He decided now would be a good time to set her straight, to drop the bomb of how callous he could be. "Frankly, I don't even know if I'm going to be able to keep the dog."

"That's how I felt after the first few nights with Bobbi," she remembered fondly. "Not the keeping part of course. But worn-out, frazzled, in-over-my-head."

She didn't say it, but he heard it. *Alone.* He was developing a deep resentment for Blair Starr. For the way the man had made Linda feel then, for how far-reaching Blair's self-centeredness was. Blair probably wouldn't keep this dog. It would get in the way of *his* life, it would require something of him.

So, now Rick found himself committing to keeping the dog, on the spot, just to prove a point, if only to himself. As if the dog was telepathic, he raced over and tugged on the shoelace of the sneakers donned so hastily Rick had not tied them. The pup looked up at Rick, wagging his tail and wiggling.

"Okay, okay, you're here for good."

"I guess you'd better name him then," she said, as if she had never once thought the dog was not here for good.

He found himself smiling. Who else could make standing out on the lawn with at four in the morning feel like this? As if you were alive, instead of half dead from lack of sleep? As if it was a great time to discuss puppy names, weather, the state of the world, the O'Brian house. *Why are you here?* seemed to be a question getting further away, rather than closer.

"Any suggestions for names?" he asked.

"He's going to be huge. So Tiny or Midget would be cute."

"You're warped. Besides, I was definitely not thinking cute." At least not in the context of the dog. "More like Rex or Rover."

"You're unimaginative."

Well, actually, he wasn't. He was doing a pretty good job of imagining her pajamas under that jacket, and with the tiniest encouragement his mind could probably imagine off another layer of her clothing.

"So, I guess you're probably wondering what I'm

doing here?" She was scuffing her toe with interest. He noticed she was wearing slippers, not shoes.

Actually that question had slipped his mind, and he was a little sorry it had put in a reappearance, because the tone of the evening changed dramatically. Linda looked wildly uncomfortable.

"From your attire, I assumed your house was on fire," he kidded her, trying to persuade the uncomfortable look to go away.

She smiled, but was bent on confession now. "I had a dream about the dog."

"Oh?" Nothing could have surprised him more. Linda did not seem like the kind of woman who would be guided by her dreams. On the other hand, not so long ago he had caught her laying in the dewy grass in her pajamas looking at birds.

The dog did his business, and even Rick was not disciplined enough to look after that tonight. "You want to come in? Tell me about it? I don't think I was going back to sleep any time soon."

"No, that's okay." She looked down at where the pajamas poked out of her jacket, adjusted the jeans where they were binding over the cumbersome double layer.

"It's not okay. You're here. It must have been important to you. Come in."

She looked at her car wistfully, took a deep, determined breath and followed him into the house. He moved down the darkened hallway and flipped on the kitchen light. The dog raced over to his water dish and slurped back the entire contents.

"You would not believe how much pee he is now capable of manufacturing," Rick said, and was rewarded with her laughter. "Let me take your coat."

"Oh." She clutched it a little tighter around herself.

"I can already clearly see you have your pajamas on underneath it, and I've seen them before. I'm not exactly dressed myself."

She surrendered the jacket. The pajamas were as he remembered them—ridiculous, sexy.

"What are you going to do with, ah , Fido, when you have to go to work?"

Ah. They were back to the dog. Linda was certainly not anxious to discuss why she was here.

"Not leave him here. Look at my giraffe." He was scooping coffee into his maker, decaf, though why he was trying to be practical now he had no idea. His robe was slipping open, and he could see the exact moment she realized he was bare-chested.

She practically bolted to the living room to investigate the damage to the giraffe. "Are these tooth marks on his hooves?"

"Yeah! And what does it say about giraffe-eating dogs in the obedience book? *Nada.*"

"He just needs some of those little chew bones. Have you got some?"

"Not yet."

"Is that because you weren't expecting to be a dog owner?"

He went very still. So, finally, the reason for this visit.

"You didn't get him for you, did you, Rick?" She had

materialized at the kitchen door, leaned her shoulder against the frame, folded her arms neatly over her devils. He was aware she was studying his face. Naturally he refused to look at her.

Impatient about the coffee, he removed the pot and stuck a mug right under the dribble. "What makes you say that?"

"That's what I dreamed. That you got the dog for me."

"Okay," he said, and handed her the mug. "That's spooky."

"True?"

"Unfortunately, yes. You're scaring me. What else have you dreamed about?" He avoided looking at her lips. Or her eyes. Or those pajamas, or even *thinking* about what lie beyond the pajamas. Linda as a mind reader was a very disturbing thought.

"Why did you get me the dog, Rick?"

"Didn't the dream tell you that part?"

"No."

"Well, maybe if you go back to sleep…"

She shook her head.

He took a deep breath and decided to come clean. "Okay, I got you the dog so you could have a nice, trustworthy companion." He hesitated. "So I didn't have to find a trustworthy guy for you who met all my requirements."

She didn't look too happy about that. It had been unfortunate to admit it to her, but no guy was in his best defensive mode at—he slid a look at the clock—four-fifteen in the morning.

"So, are you happy?" he asked, even though it was

very evident she wasn't. "Is that what you came over to find out?"

"Not exactly. I mean, I thought it was all about the dog, but on the way here I realized it wasn't."

"What was it then?"

"I wanted to see if you were everything you seemed to be. Such as available."

He felt frozen with panic. That was the very thing. He wasn't available. He wanted to be but he simply wasn't. Blair had made him guardian of secrets. Rick practically had that letter memorized he had read it so often.

You have more integrity than any man I know. At times it has angered me, because it made me feel like less than you. But now, I feel grateful to have one person on the face of the earth I can trust so completely with this.

That person should have been Blair's wife, but of course the secret the letter went on to reveal made it clear why it was not. And despite how dishonorable that secret was, how it shone a beam of light on the gritty underside of Blair's world, a man's trust was a sacred thing. A dead man's trust was a heavy responsibility, as strong, as unbreakable as steel.

Speaking of spooky, Blair had delivered that letter into Rick's hands one week before he died. Blair would seem to be the man least likely to have a premonition, or to act on it if he had. But he had died, and Rick had been left holding an envelope that said *Open only in event of death.* Those circumstances had given the contents of that letter a great deal more sway over Rick than they might normally have had. In the final analysis, Rick knew Blair had been determined to do one right thing: to accept full responsibility for the well-being of the child he had fathered.

But now Rick knew things that could break Linda's heart all over again, and he simply could not be the one to do that to her. Hadn't he seen her mending over the past days and weeks? Hadn't he seen the light come back to her eyes? Hadn't he seen confidence flowing into her like life-giving water into a place that had been parched by drought?

This desire to do what was right by her, even if it cost him, was a form of love. More noble than any other form he had ever chosen.

Love.

He had deliberately not let that word enter his contemplation of his relationship with Linda. Now that it had, would he ever look at her again without hearing it in his mind, a whisper of purity and goodness?

"Brutus," he blurted out.

"Excuse me?"

"For the dog." A stupid name. A Freudian slip. A man another man had thought he could trust when he could not trust him at all.

"We are not talking about the dog's name right now!"

No, they weren't. They were talking about a man's soul.

She actually stamped her foot, and if her annoyance

wasn't directed at him, he might have found the gesture quite adorable.

"We are talking about you and about me," she said, and in the way she said it he caught sight of a woman of such confidence and strength it nearly left him breathless.

That word appeared in his mind again, unbidden. *Love.* No, it didn't just appear in his mind. He felt it in his heart and his soul. His *mind* was trying desperately to be sensible.

Into his uncomfortable silence, she spoke again, her voice spitting with outrage. "*You* got me a dog so you didn't have to find *me* a man?"

"Now, Linda—"

"Don't you *now Linda* me. Do you think I'm not capable of finding my own man, if I wanted one?"

"Ah—"

"Imagine that! I was stupid enough to think I might want you! You can't even answer a simple question. Are you available or aren't you?"

"Linda," he said uncomfortably, "maybe we should talk about this another time." Not now, not when he was weak with the knowledge that he was falling for her. And now she was telling him she felt the same way. At least, he thought that was what she was saying.

She set down the coffee. "Actually, Rick, I'm all done talking."

"You are?" He looked at her, faintly hoping that meant she was leaving and at the same time knowing he was not ready for this to be over. That's what a woman like Linda did; she divided a man against himself.

He wanted her to stay. He wanted her to go. He wanted to find another man for her. He could not find another man for her. He saw himself as splintered and imperfect, a man who was both good and bad, weak and strong, loving and selfish.

Something blazed in her eyes, fierce and tantalizing. He realized it was passion, and that she had seen his heart as clearly as if he had spoken it out loud. How could you hide anything from a woman who dreamed in truth?

"I just realized," she said with quiet determination, "that there is one way to find out exactly what I want to know. Without words getting in the way. Without our pasts complicating everything."

She took a step toward him. He knew what was coming, and he knew what he had to do about it. He set down his coffee. He had to rebuff her. But the truth— his truth—was not about to be refused.

Did he actually open his arms to her?

She came into them. His robe had fallen open a bit more, and she leaned the silk of her hair against the nakedness of his chest, and whatever remaining strength he'd possessed disappeared. His plans, his blueprint for how this was going to work, dissolved as he folded his arms around her.

Homecoming.

Nothing had ever felt quite so right as the slightness of her against him, her breath touching his chest in warm puffs. He drank in her scent and her softness. He told himself, sternly, *I will have this moment. I will savor this moment. And then I will let go.*

But when he did marshal all his strength, a lifetime of discipline, to let her go, she lifted her head and regarded him with suede-soft eyes, luminescent with her depth and her glory and her incredible spirit. She ignored the fact that he had let her go: She twined her arms around his neck and pulled him in closer. Her eyelids closed over the softness of her eyes, and she melted into him, tilted her chin and offered him her lips.

Rose petals that had captured morning dew could not have been so profoundly beautiful. He wanted her lips. He wanted to taste, to have, to savor. He wanted one more moment to sustain him through the nights that lie ahead. Nights that would be made so unbearably lonely by the discovery that he loved her. And the truth that he could not have her without hurting her.

I will have this moment, he told himself again, aware that a better man might have been able to keep his eye on the bigger plan.

He surrendered to her absolute power over him. He took what she offered. He took the softness of her lips and he drank from the sweetness of her soul. He gently plundered her: the curve of her neck; the velvet of her eyelids; the tiny jewel-like lobes of her ears. He kissed her with the appetite of a man who had waited his whole life to taste such an exquisite feast.

He took, and she gave willingly, and then the tide gently reversed. She took and he gave. With her lips, she anointed the heat of his brow and the hollow of his throat, she shattered every rational thought he had ever had, she took him to a place free of thought, smoldering with pure feeling, shimmering with potent discovery. Her curves, luscious and feminine, pressed against the nakedness of his chest. She had on absolutely nothing under those pajamas, and the sensation of being so very close to her flesh erased every single thing from his being that had existed before this moment.

"Ah," she breathed against him, as if she had discovered her deepest secrets and his, as if she knew everything that he did not. "Ah," she said, with deep conviction, as if she knew the world was a place of magic and wonder.

In that moment, in her soul sighing its knowing and surrender, he gave her what remained of his tattered control. He gave himself completely over to her.

Her hand, soft, tender, found the opening in his robe, skimmed the texture of his belly, explored his chest, tortured his nipples, stole the breath from his throat.

"I don't need a dog," she breathed.

That was perfectly evident to him.

"Rick, I need you."

The touch of his skin beneath her fingertips made her feel deliciously, wonderfully crazy. Linda knew she was behaving wantonly. But she had wanted an answer to how he felt about her, and she had sensed him getting ready to put up barriers of words and intellect and rationale. She had needed to bypass all of that. She had needed to get to what was real, and she had known the shortest path there would be through physical contact. She had succeeded beyond her wildest dreams.

Still, the back of her brain buzzed noisily. It said, *what has gotten into you?* Whooping cranes at dawn, motorcycle rides in black leather, now nocturnal forays in her pajamas. Passionate kisses. Heated touches.

She knew exactly what had gotten into her. For weeks now she had been on a journey, and it was proving to be the longest and most difficult journey of her life. It was the journey from her head to her heart.

No, she had the timeline wrong. Her journey could not be measured in recent days, weeks, or months. Possibly she could trace these changes to the questions that had nagged her since the death of her husband.

Who am I? What am I worth? What do I want? What do I want to get from life? Will the real Linda Starr please stand up?

Maybe she could even trace the first few steps of this journey back nineteen years to when she'd said "I do" to the wrong man, for all the wrong reasons. She had been, then, ruled by fear.

Sometimes it seemed almost every moment since then had been ruled by that same fear: What will people think? Since she had found herself pregnant at nineteen hadn't she gone into overdrive to prove to her parents, her friends, her husband—the whole world—that she was really a good girl? A good person? Decent, stable, reliable?

So much of her life had been about proving what she was not. She became the ideal wife to a very wealthy, successful man. She became cultured, the woman who handled herself in social situations with grace and calm and savvy. She became the ideal mother. All of it to lay to rest those voices that had once whispered behind her back, tramp. Slut. Married because they *had* to.

But had she ever been able to silence the voice within her that judged her so harshly? What part of her husband's rejection did she own? By trying to banish the girl who had let passion overcome common sense had she alienated her husband?

That familiar feeling came over her, the one she thought she had left in the rubble of broken crystal in her basement—something turned to ice within her, hard and cold and unforgiving, something that made her unwilling to look at her part in the charade of her marriage.

But thankfully, at that moment, thoughts of her past and her future were washed away but the fiercely possessive way Rick took her lips, bringing her back to him and to herself.

Here, at an ungodly hour of the morning, coffee cooling on the counter, dog snoozing in the corner, she began to tremble with sensation. And the real Linda Starr stood up—with a vengeance.

She took herself back and felt the pure power of who she was—a passionate, sensual woman. A real woman, with needs and hungers and weaknesses.

She gave herself permission to be that, to glory in his lips and his hands and the hard masculine angles of his body pressed into the curves of hers. She tasted her glory, and his, in the heat of that kiss, in the passion that sizzled in the air, unstoppable.

The green of his eyes had darkened to a shade she had never seen before, inky, mysterious, compelling.

His lips on hers became less tender and more commanding. There was a hint of something savage in the way he laid claim to her, and something in her answered with equal savagery. It was the part of her that she'd tried to deny, that she'd imprisoned in a dingy inner dungeon, but its imprisonment had not made it weak. A dragon of desire—fiercely strong, ultimately untamable—burst free of its chains.

Rick pulled back, his breath coming in ragged gasps, and looked deep into her eyes. She saw the question, appreciated the effort it took him to ask instead of to just take.

Trembling, she nodded her assent.

He spoke, his voice hoarse with longing. "Linda, are you sure?"

Her name on his lips sounded like a blessing. She was sure. He took her hand and led her up the stairs to a gorgeous loft room. One wall was a bank of windows that looked toward the inky black of the Bow. The same river that ran by her own house, where she had seen the crane. The water, life-giving and mysterious, joined their lives together.

His room was beautiful, clean and spacious and open. The enormous bed was perfectly made—linens crisp and white, the feather duvet folded neatly at the bottom. He led her to that bed and laid her on it. He shrugged out of his robe. He was naked from the waist up, low-slung pajama pants clinging to the jut of his hips.

Her breath stopped.

She had forgotten the pure and magnificent beauty of a man. Moonlight streamed in that huge window, glanced off his chest. He came toward her, but she held up her hand. No. Just to look, for a moment longer, to drink him in.

She took in the wideness of his shoulders, the sculpted perfection of his chest, the flat hardness of his belly. She looked at the powerful lines of his face and at the light that burned in his eyes. It was like a dream. Or a painting—him, frozen in moonlight.

Then he came to her. He leaned over her and nibbled her ear. His hand found the tender swell of her breast, and the dragon within her roared its need. Then whimpered with it. And the dream ended, too soon.

The phone rang, shrill and jangling.

"Ignore it," he growled into her ear. "No good ever came from a phone ringing in the darkest hours of the night." His voice was sending as many shivers down her spine as his kisses had. He put his mouth to her neck and nuzzled until she thought she would scream with tension.

She pushed him away, the phone making her crazy, making her remember she had a daughter who might call her in the dark of the night. Bobbi would be worried if she called and her mother was not at home. The ringing of that phone was drawing Linda back to the woman she had been for so long—the responsible one everyone could rely on.

If her daughter called and her mother was not home who would she call next? Rick, of course, her godfather.

"What if that's Bobbi?" Linda whispered.

"Bobbi?" He scowled, obviously not following a

parent's logic. He didn't know how one's first thoughts flew to the possibility that something had happened...

He reached for the phone, picked it up, growled an unfriendly, "Yeah?"

She watched his face, saw the quick glance her way. She could hear a woman's voice on the other end of the phone but knew, with sick intuition, it was not Bobbi.

Rick cast another glance her way. "I'll call you right back."

She closed her eyes and felt the passion drain from her to be replaced with an infinite weariness. She remembered this scenario all to well. Mysterious phone calls in the night.

He hung up the phone and turned to her, his chest heaving. He ran a hand through his rumpled hair. Crazily she noticed his rooster tail, and she wished she had touched it again while she had the chance.

"Sorry," he said.

Even if his voice had not been loaded with guilt, she would have seen it in his eyes. He was not going to offer any explanation about that phone call.

She got up off the bed, forcing a chipper note into her voice. In her own ears her voice sounded brittle and ready to break. "No, don't be sorry. Thank God that happened! Saved by the bell."

She wished he would argue with her, say *saved?* in an indignant tone of voice, push her back onto the bed, make her world all right again.

But he didn't. The phone call had changed everything.

"Rick," she said, "forget this ever happened."

She ran for the door, and he didn't follow her. When she glanced back, he was sitting on the edge of the bed, his hands laced together, looking at the floor.

He was not about to forget it ever happened.

And, neither, unfortunately, was she.

CHAPTER EIGHT

RICK heard her go down the steps and out the front door. He heard her little car purr to life and leave.

He cradled his head in his hands, ashamed. He had seen the look in her eyes after he had set down the phone. He would have done anything to reassure her it was not what she thought. But that wasn't really true—it may not have been precisely what she thought, but it was close enough.

She was a woman from whom the worst of secrets had been kept.

And that is what he had seen in her eyes—that she knew, absolutely, and beyond a shadow of a doubt. She knew he had kept a secret from her.

She probably thought it was another woman. The real secret would probably be far more devastating to her than that.

The call had come from Tracy. She was very young to have shouldered the responsibility of taking on guardianship of her niece, her sister's child. Her sister and Blair Starr's child. Sometimes she did that, called in the night, less now than she had at first. But she was scared and alone with that baby, and he had always made it a point to be there for her.

Now he wondered why she had called—was it an emergency? Even though it felt as if his limbs were made of lead, as if he was so weary he could not speak, he forced himself to call her back.

"Sorry," he said, "I was busy."

"Oh," she said, sounding unreasonably happy that he had been *busy* at that hour. "I shouldn't have called you. Angelina has been crying for hours, I didn't know what to do."

He could hear the baby crying in the background, little exhausted hiccupping sobs.

"Tracy when the baby cries for that long, take her to the hospital. Why didn't you?"

"That's why I phoned. I had tried to get a cab, but it didn't come. I was hoping you would take me."

He wanted to yell at her. She should have called an ambulance. But he bit his tongue. His irritation had nothing to do with Tracy. Nothing at all. His sense of shame deepened. He was not going to be the man Linda deserved if everything was always all about him.

He was thinking about Linda as if they had a future, with a certain measure of optimism, given what had just happened between them. Which meant he had to clear this mess up, and the sooner the better.

Forcing himself to do one thing at a time, he listened hard to Tracy's soft voice as she described the baby's symptoms. He heard what she wasn't saying. She was scared to go to the hospital by herself.

Tracy was sweet and gentle, a wonderful parental figure for the baby. But she was young and uneducated and had very little confidence. He suspected even a trip to the emergency ward would rattle her. She was easily intimidated. Most people, if a cab they had ordered didn't come, would have phoned back and complained.

"I'll be right over," he said. "We'll go now."

"Thank you."

He got up and got dressed, looked at his bed and allowed himself for one brief moment to think of what had almost happened there. Then he forced himself to move on. Hours later, he dropped Tracy and Angelina back at the small house Blair's money had allowed them to have, that Rick had personally selected for them. Angelina was sleeping, finally, on a strong dose of antibiotics.

He went to his office. No one was in yet, but he left his secretary a note to cancel all his appointments for the day. Then he made a new one.

His friend Laurence met him for breakfast at a quiet downtown café where they could have the privacy of a booth. They had been friends since school. Laurence was a lawyer now whose firm handled all the legal work for Star Chasers. His firm had not handled setting up the trust for Tracy and Angelina.

"You look like hell," Laurence said without preamble.

"I am in hell," he said. "Can I show you something?"

"As a friend or a client?"

"Friend." He passed him the letter from Blair, that

last letter, that seemed to be changing the course of Rick's whole life.

Laurence had known Blair, too, but as he read the letter a frown deepened around his mouth. "You couldn't know Blair and not like him," he said, looking up from the letter, "but what a scoundrel. I mean, okay, he's looking after the kid, but what a thing to do to Linda. I take it you've followed his instructions to the letter, and she doesn't know about this?"

"That's why I need your advice," Rick said.

Laurence's eyes were sharp on his face. The waitress brought them coffee, neither of them ordered breakfast.

"Something is going on between you and Linda," Laurence guessed. His skill at reading people was nothing short of phenomenal.

"I'm in love with Linda."

"Ah, the plot thickens. So, I'll tell you my professional opinion. This is not a legal document. It is in no way binding," Laurence said.

Rick said nothing, twirled his coffee cup in his hands, waiting for a feeling of relief to come, but it didn't. The legalities of the situation were not the issue. Legal matters were black and white. Matters of the heart and soul were not quite so cut-and-dried.

"Now, I'll give you a personal opinion, as your friend, whether you want to hear it or not."

Rick wanted to hear it.

"Leaving you this letter, and this kind of responsibility, was the action of a totally self-centered, irresponsible son of a bitch."

"Is that a legal term?" Rick asked.

Laurence ignored him. "He put you in this position without your permission. You're acting as if you consented to keep his dirty secrets, but you didn't."

Rick thought of the sweet baby with her round face and blond curls that he had brought to the hospital this morning. He didn't like Angelina being referred to as anybody's dirty little secret, but he knew there was no point in clarifying. Angelina was not really the issue.

"He trusted me with this because he knew what kind of man I was. Am," Rick amended hastily.

"Yeah, a sucker," Laurence said, and then softened it. "Hey, you have a good heart. He took advantage of that."

"So, what next?"

Laurence smiled slightly. "You don't need me to tell you what's next. You know what to do."

"I need to tell her," Rick said and as soon as he said the words out loud he knew that he had known that for a long time. And he knew that the reason he hadn't told her was out of loyalty to Blair, but because Rick hated to be the one to hurt her. What she didn't know could only hurt her more.

Laurence confirmed that. "Okay, I'm glad that's your decision, because even though I'm assuming Blair has provided generously for the child, who knows? Someday, someone might advise the kid to go for a bigger piece of the pie. Think of what a shock that would be to Linda."

Rick did think of it, and didn't like it one little bit.

"And would Angelina be entitled to it? A bigger piece of the pie?"

"The kind of question that lawyers get very rich trying to answer. Now lighten up. For a man in love you're looking mighty grim."

"Because it's so damn complicated."

"Well, get used to it buddy, because that's what love is."

Laurence was right.

When Rick dropped by the O'Brian house to see Linda, to arrange a time to meet with her, she wasn't there. He felt a little sick. Was she not there because of what had happened last night? She'd be at home, nursing her wounds, probably downing chocolate chip cookies at a scary rate.

"You want to have a look around?" Jason asked. "It's good, even for us." He grinned cockily.

The house looked extraordinary. New floors gleamed, the transitions to the old floors were seamless. For the walls Linda had chosen colors off the historic color wheel, and Rick was amazed by what she had unearthed: beautiful rich shades of gold and sensuous burgundies. Drapes and window treatments accentuated the beauty of the stained glass uppers in the windows and the amazing patina of the refurbished wood sills. She'd used subtle techniques to draw attention to the dramatic height of the ceilings and their plaster detail. The kitchen was magazine-layout perfect—stainless steel appliances, black marble counter tops, sleek light fixtures—and yet the spirit of the room, its history and its dignity, were completely intact. The old pantry—an entire room of shelves and storage off the kitchen—had been updated, but kept in its entirety.

The house shone with her love. Her heart and her soul was everywhere.

"You've got to see the master bath," Jason said. "It's the best work I've ever done."

"Actually," Rick looked at his watch, "I don't have time." But the truth was he did not want to see the finished master bath.

"She's planning an open house," Jason said. "I bet it sells that day. *I'm* even in love with the old gal."

He was going to punch Jason in the mouth. Linda? The old gal? It was exactly what he'd tried to warn her about!

"The house," Jason said, almost gently, "I was talking about the house."

"So where is Linda right now?"

He braced himself, knowing what was coming. She'd called in sick. Sounded like she had a bad cold—the sound of a woman who had cried all night.

"I think she said she was going to her motorcycle riding lesson. That's cool, huh?"

If she was nursing any kind of wound at all, she was managing to fit it into a very busy schedule.

When he finally caught her on her cell phone her voice didn't sound muffled or sniffly at all. She informed him that because of the upcoming open house, the best she could do was squeeze him in for a quick dinner the night before the big unveiling.

"Look, Linda, about last night—"

"I seem to be breaking up," she said, and the line went dead.

He glared at it. He should have pushed for an earlier

meeting. He hadn't because he knew he needed time to figure out exactly what to say. So while he brooded and debated, she seemed to be having the time of her life. The whole office was buzzing about the soiree she was planning for the O'Brian house. It was quickly turning into the social event of the season.

"She has a connection with the Calgary barbershop quartet champions. They were going to offer up period songs on the front porch," one of his secretaries told him. "And I'm ordering the canapés from Fernando's. Imagine them agreeing to do it. It takes a month to get a table there for dinner! And that gorgeous antique shop on 17th— Past Lives—is donating furniture for the day. No charge."

Rick happened to know that her connection with the barbershop quartet was a baritone named Herbert who had been friends with Blair. As had Fernando. No doubt the antique shop was also owned by a man who was available. They were all circling her like hawks after a sparrow. Or maybe she was the hawk, and they were the sparrows, falling helplessly from the sky in the face of that understated charm and grace of hers, slain by it, just as he had been.

Meanwhile, what was his life? Potty-training a dog. He'd been informed the dog would be too large for the condo. The puppy had taken to howling whenever Rick was forced to leave him alone, locked in the bathroom where he could do the least damage. Rick had received complaints. His lovely neighbor, Mildred's evil twin, was muttering that the grass would come up dead in the places where the dog was helpfully watering it.

Tonight, Rick got home to find he had been hand-delivered a letter from the condo committee, snotty in tone, telling him a lapdog was acceptable and naming some breeds that would be fine.

He looked at the list, bemused. A Jack Russell terrier? A miniature poodle? Those were not manly dogs.

He tossed the list and put his dog on his lap, looking at his huge paws with approval. He could hardly believe he had once considered giving *his* dog to Linda, or giving him up. The dog was a very nice distraction from the mess of his life. The dog required maintenance, food, water and walks, and poop patrol. For that Rick was eternally grateful.

"I'm not trading you in for a Jack Russell," he said.

The dog, still unnamed, moaned his approval as Rick found the sweet spot under his chin.

"They can't tell me what breed of dog to own. Police state."

He fell asleep on the couch with his dog. Somehow his bed had become unbearable.

The night he was supposed to meet Linda at a quiet little lounge in Eau Claire, she called, sounding genuinely frazzled.

"Rick, I am utterly exhausted. I've been arranging furniture all day, and the florist got the order mixed up. I have all the funeral flowers for someone named Bertie Cuthbertson. And one of the barbershop quartet guys has strep throat."

"It must be going around," he said. Uncharitably he hoped Herbert was suffering.

He knew Linda was exhausted. She was practically putting on a three-ring circus all by herself. And squeezing in motorcycle lessons. Still, it was her own fault. Had she even once called him and asked for help? Besides, he was exhausted, too, his nerves frayed with the weight of carrying two secrets.

One about Blair's daughter.

The second about Rick's love for Linda.

Maybe confession wasn't such a good idea. He knew he had to see her now, before he talked himself out of this.

"Could I just drop by your place? I don't think it will take long."

"Sure," she said, but she didn't sound sure at all, and the memory of the last time they had been alone together leaped across the telephone line.

No cookies this time. No defense at all.

And when she opened the door, he understood why the O'Brian house was filling up with free antiques, why Fernando was providing the snacks, why Herbert, pre-strep throat, had planned to sing his heart out.

For her.

They were doing it for her, because her loveliness was astonishing.

It had done nothing but grow ever since she had taken on that house. With the rebirth of the house, her own beauty had been restored. And he hoped what he was about to say wasn't going to change that.

"Come in," she said.

Somewhere in her busy schedule, she'd had time to arrange her living room. It was cozy and inviting, as if she had spent a lot of time on it, which hopefully meant not too much time for the hawks.

She'd also had time to do something to her hair. It had blond streaks in it and had grown past the spiky stage. Her eyes were made-up beautifully and looked as glamorous as those of a movie star. She was wearing a cream silk suit with a black clingy tank underneath it. Jewels shone at her ears and her throat.

"Coffee?" she asked him when he'd settled. The expression on her face, helped by the makeup and the super suave outfit, was faintly remote—reminded him of when she'd been Blair's wife. He wanted to strip that mask from her.

With his lips.

Not with the words he was about to speak. He shook his head to the coffee. "Please sit down."

Puzzled, she did so.

"I have something very hard to tell you."

She looked as if she wanted to get up and run away, but she folded her hands primly in her lap, a woman prepared for the worst.

"When the phone rang the other night, I know you assumed I had a girlfriend or was seeing someone else. Nothing could be further from the truth."

"Really, Rick," she said coolly, not the passionate woman she had been that night at all, "that's your business. You don't have to—"

"Linda, it was a girl named Tracy Addison."

He saw the last name register slightly.

"Lacy Addison's sister," he said softly.

"The woman Blair died with," she said, her voice like wood.

He nodded.

"I saw her picture in the paper. Right beside Blair's under the headline, Two Calgarians Die in Fire. She was very beautiful."

Her voice was remote, her eyes hooded.

"Um, Tracy isn't much like her."

"Tracy and Lacy. How cute." Her voice was cold. "And you have a relationship with that woman's sister because?"

That woman.

He had thought about this and rehearsed it, and thought about it some more. But there was simply no easy way to say it.

"That woman," he said carefully, "Lacy, had a baby. Tracy is her guardian. The baby's name is Angelina."

Linda looked at him without comprehension. He realized he was going to have to spell it out very, very clearly.

"Lacy and Blair had a baby," he said softly.

The coolness faded from her face, and she looked at him with a numb lack of understanding. Then it seemed to hit her swiftly, like a blow to the stomach. She folded up, soundless, rocking, her mouth moving, but not a sound coming out.

He was at her side in a moment, but she pushed him away, would not allow him to offer her comfort.

"I wanted more babies," she finally choked out, and

her voice was a terrible thing to hear, ice cracking with pain. "I wanted a bigger family. He wouldn't...he wouldn't even discuss it."

"I'm so sorry, Linda."

She straightened. Her eyes were dry, but sparked with the same ice he'd heard in her voice.

"Why didn't you tell me before now?" she asked after a long time.

He wanted to blame Blair, but he knew he could not. "I didn't want to hurt you any more than you had already been hurt. I thought maybe you wouldn't really want to know."

She was silent. She didn't look at him. Her hands were clasped together, and they were white around the knuckles.

"And why didn't you tell me about Blair?" she asked, finally, softly, proudly. When she asked the question, he realized it had been there, unspoken, between them all along. She threw up her head and looked at him. "Everybody knew. Why wasn't there ever a whisper, or an anonymous phone call? Why?"

He gathered his courage. "Linda, you didn't want to know about Blair."

"Excuse me?" She tilted her chin, and he saw her knuckles grow whiter.

"He told you. He told you in every single way except the words. He told you when he didn't come home at night, and when he left for weekends without you. He told you when you found phone numbers in his pockets and lipstick on his collars. He told you."

Silence, and then a deep shudder. He went to touch

her, to put his hand around her shoulder, but she flinched away from him, and he let his hand drop away.

"This other news? I felt you had a right to know. I didn't know how you and I could ever move forward if I knew and you didn't. But, Linda, it really doesn't have to affect you."

Linda stared at Rick, feeling as if his voice was coming to her from a long way away. This news didn't have to affect her? How could it not? Blair had refused her more children. He had kept her from the life she wanted for herself. Just as surely as she had kept him from the one he had wanted for himself.

"Bobbi has a sister," she said carefully. "How can that possibly not affect me?"

The bitterness rose in her like bile. Not just this news, but his other words. *Linda, you didn't want to know about Blair.*

"I need to be alone," she said. "Thank you for coming by."

"Linda—"

If he didn't go, she might look at the gentleness in his eyes and be weakened by it. This pain that ate at her belly was truth, and she did not want him trying to take it away from her. It was her shield and her defense.

Rick's leaving was a blur.

When he was gone, she went into the basement and found a whole box of dishes she had not yet broken. She wanted to fling each thing Blair had ever touched at the wall until it was all broken beyond repair, but she knew it wouldn't help. Because there was something he had touched that was already broken beyond repair. Her.

She crawled into bed. She did not even have the energy to undress herself. Before she slept she thought of the kindness in Rick's face. And then of his words, absolving himself and everyone else of the crime that had been committed against her.

Linda, you didn't want to know about Blair.

How good tears would have felt, but they did not come. Linda wished she felt something, but she felt nothing at all except weak gratitude for the open house in the morning. Without it she might have crawled into a hole and never come out. But the next day she had, by the grace of God, no time to wallow in self-pity. None at all.

Mildred, dressed more beautifully than a queen, thankfully saw herself as the true hostess of the affair. She led tours and talked about the history of the house, told wonderful anecdotes about weddings and summer picnics on the lawn. It left Linda to busy herself with details: opening more wine, refreshing the canapé plates, refilling glasses.

The day was absolutely gorgeous—one of those mild fall days where the sun washed the world in gold. The house filled with laughter and the sound of clinking glasses, people talking. The crowd spilled out into the yard and the party lasted well past the posted time.

The Barbershop Boys had found a replacement for the sick singer, and though they had only agreed to perform half a dozen songs, they sang for the pure joy of singing, and they didn't stop. The beautiful harmonies from days gone by drifted from the porch across the lawns and up through the house. The last of the guests departed to the soft, haunting notes of "Goodnight, Irene."

Hours later, darkness had fallen, the caterers were gone, and Linda took the last garbage bag out the back door. Only Mildred remained.

Rick had not come, though she had waited for him and watched for him. More evidence, as if she needed any, that the only person she should ever rely on was herself.

"Come on, Mildred, I'll drive you home."

"Linda?"

"Yes?"

"Thank you. This was one of the best days of my life."

"I'm so glad," Linda said, and she meant it. No matter what she was feeling, her life could still have meaning, she could still be of service, she could still give moments of joy to others. *Perhaps I'll become a nun,* she thought, and the fact that a small smile formed inside of her was another little glimpse of hope.

But after she'd dropped Mildred off at the seniors' complex, Linda felt herself drawn back to the O'Brian house. She let herself in the front door, turned on the lights and went through it slowly. She loved every room and every fixture and every piece of wood.

She stopped in that incredible bathroom, touched the tub. She could feel tears filming her eyes. How silly that she could cry over a house that was not hers, but not shed a single tear over her dead husband's treachery. How silly of her to have become so attached to this house, to have pictured herself living in each of these rooms, bathing in this tub, making cookies in that kitchen.

Or maybe not so silly. Houses, things, had no power to hurt, to wound.

She heard the front door open, the footsteps, strong and masculine coming through the house with no hesitation at all. He knew exactly where to find her, but she refused to turn when she heard him come into the room, refused to let the happiness that wanted to take wing within her fly.

She knew this moment belonged to both of them. Because he was part of this house as much as she was, a part of the incredible metamorphosis that had happened to her here.

"Linda," he said quietly, "the house sold."

So much for the idea that the house could not hurt her. She hated that it had sold so quickly. That she couldn't come back here, whenever she wanted, and take comfort from the solidness of these walls.

She tried to manufacture a happy note, but her voice trembled. "I knew that might happen."

"You made a name for yourself today," he said. "The sky's the limit, now."

Funny, how it didn't feel that way at all.

"Linda, I have to tell you something."

She turned, for the first time. He looked faintly haggard, and his rooster tail was sticking up even more than normal. She folded her treacherous hands across her chest.

"I bought the house. Personally. From Star Chasers management."

Her mouth fell open. "You what?"

"I needed it for the dog," he said, a trifle defensively. "He has to have a yard. The neighbors over at the condo are getting ugly about him."

She stared at him, not knowing whether to laugh or cry. Rick had bought the house? For his dog? What kind of man did that kind of wonderful, crazy, beautiful thing?

Instead of saying that, she turned away from him, and said, "Are you ever going to name that poor dog?"

He sighed. "I keep thinking I'll know when the right name comes to me. I even try some of them out, but nothing clicks. This week he's been called Alfie, Mickey and Bartholomew."

"You're right. None of them is quite right."

He came to her, refusing to let her keep her back to him. He looked down into her eyes. He touched her cheek with his hand, and she leaned in to it, closed her eyes and allowed herself to feel what it was to be with Rick: safe, cherished, able to trust.

She pulled away because feeling those things made her so vulnerable.

"I don't think," he said softly, "that I really bought the house for the dog."

She dared not speak.

"I think I bought it because for the first time in a long, long time, I want to believe in the future. I want to believe in a future for us."

"Oh, Rick," she said sadly. Only a week ago hadn't

she been pressing him for this? Wanting to know exactly where she stood with him? Now, she could see how he felt in his eyes.

"I know you're absolutely raw with the news that Blair had a baby, Linda. I know that. But I want you to know, I'll wait for you. I'll wait for you to be ready."

She felt the tears clawing at her throat and pushed them back, fiercely. She didn't want to cry anymore. She didn't want to be soft and vulnerable. Yet to allow herself to love Rick, to be a woman worthy of being loved by him, she had to be those things.

"You don't have to say a word," he said softly. "Not one word. All you have to do is let me carry you through this."

It was what she had wanted her entire life. Someone she could lean on. Someone to be strong. Someone to take away the ache of loneliness within her. But now that it was being offered, she didn't know what to do with it.

"Let's just take it nice and slow," he said easily. "No rushing, just one small step at a time."

"Beginning where?" she asked.

"I could use some help moving. And I'll need someone to bake cookies with. So it smells like home."

She had barely known Blair when she had stood beside him at an altar and promised till death do us part.

This time she could go slowly.

She put her hand in Rick's, and he kissed her tenderly on the cheek.

The next weeks went by in a lovely slow motion blur. She and Rick found a new house for Star Chasers to purchase. It was not the O'Brian house, but it was a lovely 1930s style bungalow in the more middle class Killarney-Glengarry area.

She took her motorcycle lessons. They went out for dinners, and took the dog for lovely rambling walks through some of Calgary's most wonderful parks— Glenmore, Sandy Beach, Nose Hill, Fish Creek. She felt like she was rediscovering the city where she had grown up.

The pain ebbed. Rick was everything a woman could ever hope for. Tender, reliable, loyal, passionate, fun. And yet something in her held back.

The week before Thanksgiving he gave her a ring.

She stared at the beautiful box, traced the simplicity of the diamond with her fingertips. It was not the kind of ring that Blair would have bought. There was nothing showy about it.

The ring spoke of Rick's heart: strong and uncomplicated.

She felt so honored and so blessed that a man like Rick could love her as much as he did. It was in every little gesture. In the cute notes he left on her car and the sweet messages he left on her machine. It was in the flowers that were delivered to her door and the small and wonderful gestures of consideration he made every single day.

She looked at the ring and at him.

He closed his hand over hers, smiled at her with absolutely no impatience.

"Don't say no," he whispered. "Just think about it."

And she promised that she would. But then she heard those words again, like an accusation, an arrow to her heart. *Linda, you didn't want to know about Blair.* She gave the ring back.

CHAPTER NINE

THE ringing of the phone was shrill and incessant. Rick Chase started awake. The red digits on his bedside clock flashed 4:00 a.m.

No good ever came from a phone ringing in the darkest hours of the night.

He picked up the receiver, aware he was braced for the worst and hoping for a drunk who had dialed the wrong number.

"Hello?"

"Uncle Rick?"

The last vestiges of sleep were gone. He sat up in bed, the blankets falling away from his naked chest. He fumbled for the light on his night table, as if being able to see would help him hear better.

"Bobbi?"

"Sorry to wake you. I wanted to talk to you before I went to class."

"Haven't we done this before?" Rick asked sleepily. He looked around the room he was in, sometimes still disoriented by his new surroundings.

He had chosen not to sleep in the master bedroom. He was aware he was saving it, for a special night with the woman he hoped would be his bride. One day. When she was ready.

"Mommy told me a few days ago. About the baby. I haven't been able to sleep very well since."

"I'm sorry."

"Uncle Rick, I've given this a lot of thought. I want to meet her. She's my sister."

Only someone under the age of twenty would think a few days construed a lot of thought, but he let it go.

He contemplated how these late night phone calls had the effect of earthquakes, shaking up his well-ordered world. On the other hand, what had a well-ordered world ever given him? A passport thoroughly stamped with all the places he had been to, alone. With a sigh of resignation, Rick Chase decided to give up on a well-ordered life in favor of one full of surprises.

"Have you talked to your mom about it?" he asked carefully.

"She said you would know what to do."

He thought about that, Linda giving him her fragile trust on a matter that was so delicate and so important.

"Okay," he said. "You're coming home for Thanksgiving, right?"

"Next weekend!"

"I'll see what I can do."

"Uncle Rick?"

"Hmm?"

"Is something wrong with my mom?"

"What makes you ask?" Again, he was aware of something careful in his voice.

"It's just that for a while when I talked to her she seemed so happy, happier than I've ever heard her sound before. Like after you took her motorcycle riding. You should have heard her talk about that. Honestly, you would have thought she was sixteen and in love!"

He smiled at the picture that conjured, and then at the memory of that beautiful day with Linda. He was so glad that he had given it to her, so hopeful there would be many more.

But he had noticed the change in her, too. She was subdued rather than invigorated. She could be with him, and yet not with him at all, remote, as if she was behind a wall of glass where she could observe everything but nothing could touch her.

He had known, when he had chosen to tell her the truth, that it could be a risky business. People assumed that honesty was always the best policy, but he was not so sure. Could some wounds be too deep to heal?

He hoped not. He wanted a chance to give her happiness, like what she had given him. Yes, he had done things for Linda—the motorcycle ride, the job—but it was important what she had done for him. She had given him back his heart and his soul. She had breathed color back into a life gone black and white.

"Whatever I heard in her voice is gone," Bobbi said. "I miss it, even though that's the part of her I never knew very well. I don't want it to go away."

"Neither do I," Rick said quietly, and realized, when there was a long silence that he had said too much.

"Are you in love with her?" Bobbi breathed.

The phone call was beginning to feel a little too much like a late night hen party—filled with the confidences one did not share in the light of the day. Still, this was a family that had lived with half-truths and no truths at all. Bobbi would see it the minute she saw him looking at Linda anyway.

"Yes," he said. "I'm in love with your mother."

There was another long silence and then a sigh. "Cool."

He interpreted that as delight over the budding of middle-aged romance, and she confirmed it by saying, "Oh, Uncle Rick, you've made me so happy."

Why, why, why did women cry when they were happy?

"Bobbi?"

"Hmm?"

"Next time you call, could you try to remember the time difference?"

Sniffles and giggles. "Okay, Uncle Rick."

He hung up the phone. The dog had crept up on the bed during the night and now opened one sly eye to see if he'd been noticed. When he saw he had been, he whimpered, licked Rick's hand with frank adoration, shuffled his position slightly and went right back to sleep. The dog was living up to the promise of his feet. The cuteness of his puppy days were already fast fading, and he was becoming rangy, his long legs not quite fitting his pudgy body, black curly fluff turning to coarse straight black hair.

He was also still unnamed. Rick had tried Zack and

Blackie and Zamboni. Linda had given him a book called "Best Baby Names" last week, but even with thousands to choose from none felt right.

"Try starting with A," Linda had suggested. "Maybe he'll recognize his own name."

It sounded pretty whimsical to Rick. A dog would recognize his own name? He'd teased her about crystals and horoscopes, but he knew she saw things in her dreams, so maybe he should listen to her.

So he'd tried Aaron, Abdullah, Abel, Abner, Abraham. Though Rick had thought Abner might just do, the dog ignored all the names equally. He responded more readily to "hey you," and several variations of poop-head.

Rick looked at the clock and got out of bed. The dog grumbled and rolled over, taking the whole bed for himself, and Rick went across the hallway into his home office. He settled at his desk. He loved this room with its big bank of new windows facing the side yard. The room was richly masculine with wainscotting and deep brown walls and wooden window treatments. It almost felt as if Linda had been thinking of him when she had come up with the colors and the design.

Rick had liked his condo, but he now felt his heart had recognized this house as home from the minute he had first looked at it. And Mildred seemed to realize his good intentions now, too.

She came by almost daily, just for a few minutes. She was never intrusive and always came bearing a small gift: a casserole, freshly baked muffins, today a framed photo of a 1930s garden party in the very side yard this window overlooked. But his favorite gift was the way she touched his cheek, as if he were her son, and the look in her eyes when he opened the door for her. His love for the place only deepened as he discovered a friendship with Mildred and the daily little "Linda" touches everywhere. Linda's presence was in the plaid-lined shelves of the pantry, in the light switch plates in each room, in the subtle designs she had used on the walls using very faint variations of paint.

Last week she had presented him with sunshine-yellow cushions for his sofa, a framed picture of the dog for his office, a potted sunflower in bloom for the wide window ledge in the kitchen. She was managing to be "in" this house without being in it, and he was both grateful and frustrated.

It was time to take another chance, he decided, to lay all his cards on the table. He wrote out a careful list. In the morning he drove over to the new house where Linda was working.

Her car was parked outside, and so was Jason's truck. A huge Dumpster already full of broken drywall and old cabinets took up most of the small front yard.

Linda came out of the house, a nose and mouth mask covering half her face, carrying some broken pieces of Sheetrock. She was, he knew, literally throwing herself into her work. He understood that. He had used work as a balm in his own times of trouble.

"Hey," he said.

She pulled down the mask. "Hi." Her greeting wasn't unwelcoming. It was just that *something* was missing.

Her facade of complete composure was in place, just as it had been when she was married.

She wanted to be untouchable, but he knew how much pain that facade hid.

"I'm up to C for the dog."

A little light of laughter came on in her eyes. "And?"

A little was better than nothing at all. "An ear twitch for Cletus."

"You are not calling that dog Cletus."

It was his turn to laugh at her indignation. "Now why do you care what I call my dog, Linda Starr?"

"I don't. Call him whatever you want."

But he knew she did care what he called the dog, he hoped because she wanted to be part of his life. He hoped she was going to have to live with what he called the dog for a long, long time.

"Cletus, it is then," he teased her, and she thumped him on the arm, just as he hoped she would.

"I'll give you a dozen chocolate chip cookies if you don't call him that."

"Ah, so you care after all," he said softly, and saw the truth flash through her eyes, that she cared about more than what he called the dog. She yearned to come home to him. "Two dozen," he negotiated.

"Done."

"I actually dropped by to invite you for Thanksgiving dinner. It seemed like it might be a good way to christen my new place. The smell of turkey roasting has to be right up there with the smell of chocolate chip cookies baking."

"Oh!" Something wistful crossed her features. "I'd

love to, but Bobbi will be home. I invited Jason to our place—to meet her." She blushed. "She'll hate me for this."

See? She could say she didn't want to believe in love and she could try to harden her heart, but it was plain to him that part of her wanted more than anything to believe in the miracle and magic of the two right people meeting each other.

"Actually she already said she'd come to my place."

Linda put her hands on her hips. "You're stealing my daughter for Thanksgiving?"

"Jason can come, too."

"Well, I must admit it sounds delightful. That house was made for big family gatherings." That something wistful was in her eyes again, but she tried to hide it. "Though, to be honest, Rick, I really can't see you cooking a turkey."

"Humph. From a lady who has seen what I can do with a chocolate chip cookie."

"That came out of a plastic package," she reminded him.

He remembered chocolate chips on her lips and wanted nothing more than to lean toward her, erase this barrier between them. But he knew he had to be patient.

"Turkeys come wrapped in plastic, too. I checked."

She gave him another slug on the arm, and he allowed himself to savor the playful moments that he could still coax out of her.

"Mildred wants to cook my turkey," he admitted.

"Mildred?" she asked, incredulous.

"She kind of came with the house. I'm anxious to see if she can make anything besides casseroles with potato chips or cornflakes in them."

"I'd love to come," Linda decided.

"There's something else you should know." He said it carefully and casually, as if it was not a bomb he was dropping. "I've invited Tracy and Angelina."

Linda went very still.

He didn't wait for her to speak. "Bobbi wants to meet them. It seemed like the easiest way. Plus, holidays are hard on Tracy. She didn't have any family besides her sister. She and that baby are pretty much alone in the world."

He had deliberately played to her sympathy, and Linda nodded, very slowly. "All right, Rick."

For just a moment, before she looked away, he saw trust in her eyes, and he hoped beyond hope that he was going to be worthy of it.

"Mildred said be there around one," he told her.

Linda looked at herself in the mirror. She was trying way too hard. She'd had her hair styled that afternoon—new frosty highlights, not a spike in sight. The outfit was new, but it was very much what the old Linda would have worn: tan cashmere sweater, dark brown slacks, a pearl necklace and pearl studs. She looked refined and untouchable.

"Perfect," she said out loud. She did not want *that* girl's sister to see how very vulnerable she felt sharing Thanksgiving dinner with Blair's baby daughter.

But the word *perfect* hung in the air, and she looked

at her reflection again. *Linda, you didn't want to know about Blair.*

Those words that had allowed her to keep just a teensy bit of anger against Rick as a defense against his charm were true.

She was looking at the haughty reflection of a woman who hadn't wanted to know anything that would ripple the surface of her carefully constructed illusion. Linda had worked so hard to make herself and her world look absolutely perfect, and the more perfect everything had looked on the outside the more it had been falling apart on the inside.

She didn't want to be that woman in the mirror anymore. It cost too much. It took her flesh and her blood and it turned them to stone and to ice.

She backed away from the mirror and took off the outfit, even the pearls. She put on a pair of hip-hugging blue jeans that Bobbi had talked her into, a striped turtleneck, a funky scarf. No jewelry.

She met Bobbi in the hallway, and Bobbi beamed at her.

"Mom, you look so young!"

She looked at her daughter and wondered how someone could grow up so quickly. College had changed Bobbi, too, in a very short time. Her daughter was a young woman now, not her little girl anymore. Inviting Jason had probably been a mistake.

Only as it turned out, it hadn't been. Jason had arrived before them and greeted them at the door of Rick's house.

He grinned at Bobbi as if he'd known her forever. "I

call Linda *Mom,* so that must make you my sister," he said, and gave her a big brotherly bone-crushing hug.

Bobbi was introduced to Mildred, who was in the kitchen, flushed, devilishly happy to be giving Rick a hard time about the turkey he'd bought. The dog was underfoot, and Mildred ordered him locked up, muttering about creatures in the house. Linda noticed Rick took the bossiness with extraordinary good nature, locked the dog in the back porch with a wink in her direction.

The wink took her breath away. Her admission to herself—that he had been right about her not wanting to know about Blair—had taken a huge chink out of the wall she had built around herself.

She watched as Rick dealt with the dog and took turns teasing Bobbi and dodging Mildred who was trying to smack his hand with a wooden spoon as he pilfered various ingredients for supper and put them in his mouth.

Linda saw him with sudden and beautifully illuminating clarity. She saw that he had told her the truth, even when that was hard. Even when his words had hurt her. She saw that he was the rarest of men: an honest one. She did what she most needed to do: she forgave him. She forgave him for not telling her about Blair. She forgave him for being the one to bring her the news of Blair's latest treachery. She forgave him for seeing the truth about her: that she had not wanted to know.

And with that forgiveness, it felt as if she could really *see* him.

Had that been the missing piece? Had her lack of forgiveness been what had held her back?

Rick was such a truly wonderful man. She looked at him as if she had never seen him before. Like her, he'd chosen to dress causally—cords, a sweater over a shirt. He looked gloriously handsome. His rooster tail was sticking up like a flag.

"Mom, this house is incredible. You did this? You have to show me."

In a way it was a relief to pull herself away from her awareness of Rick. And just as she had seen her daughter in a new way—as a young woman and not her little girl—Bobbi saw her mother in a different way as they went through the house. She kept saying, over and over, "Mom, I had no idea."

It's okay, Bobbi, no one had any idea who I really was. Least of all me.

Bobbi stopped in the double French doorway that led from the master suite to the master bath.

"This is like something out of a dream." She turned and eyed her mother. "You did this room, too?"

Linda nodded, feeling slightly embarrassed, knowing the room said things about her that a mother did not really want her daughter to know.

"I don't really know the first thing about you, do I, Mom?"

Linda blushed wildly, and Bobbi laughed and hugged her. "I am so proud of you," she said. "You are so talented! This house is unbelievable. I'm jealous of Uncle Rick for getting to live here."

She had to get in that little dig! Bobbi had not been happy about her accommodations in her mother's guest room in the small Bow Valley house. Admittedly it was only slightly larger than a closet and had an ugly brown ring on the ceiling where the roof had leaked.

They went back downstairs and Rick mixed them all cranberry cocktails. Jason teased Bobbi unmercifully, just as an older brother would. And then the moment that Linda had been dreading arrived. The doorbell rang.

"It's them," Bobbie whispered.

Linda looked at Rick, and he mouthed something to her. She wasn't sure what. *Be strong?* Or maybe *I love you.* Whatever it was, it helped her set her shoulders and move out of the kitchen. Bobbi had flown to the front door and flung it open.

For a moment, Linda wished for the other outfit, and then was so, so glad, she had not chosen it. A child stood in the doorway, holding the hand of another child. Though Tracy was probably twenty, she looked very young and fragile. She had a loveliness about her, but none of the devil-may-care beauty that Linda had glimpsed in the photo of her sister. Tracy also looked very frightened. Clasping her hand was a tiny angel—all blond curls and blue eyes and chubby charm. The child, not quite two Rick had said, had been dressed with exquisite care, in a lovely lacy party dress, matching leotards, shiny black patent leather shoes.

"Oh," Bobbi squealed, and hugged Tracy as if she had known her forever. "I am so happy to meet you." And then she got down on her knees and opened her arms. "Hello, sis," she said gently.

Perhaps it was because the child recognized eyes as blue as her own, or perhaps hearts knew these things, but she went into Bobbi's arms as if she had been waiting her whole short life to meet this other half of her heart.

"Wow," Jason said softly. "Who the heck is that?"

Linda glanced at him. He was staring at Tracy Addison, and it was not the same look he'd had when he met Bobbi at all. He looked like a man who had just seen something he never expected to see, a man who had seen something that he hadn't ever believed was real. It was as if he had glimpsed Santa Claus coming down the chimney or the cow jumping over the moon. He moved out of the kitchen and to the front door, a man in a trance. He took Tracy's hand. Linda wondered if he was going to bend over it and kiss it!

"I'm Jason," he said, and though he refrained from the grand gesture, he held her hand way too long, and she was looking up at him as if she never wanted to let go, either.

"Well, well, well, " Rick said. He had moved beside Linda and had his hand on the small of her back. "Never saw that one coming."

Then he propelled her forward, and she was meeting Tracy, and it wasn't as bad as she had thought it would be. In fact, it wasn't bad at all. Tracy's hand was cold with nervousness, and Linda felt herself wishing warmth into the girl. They had to do the whole tour of the house again, only this time Jason was the tour guide, basking in Tracy's awed admiration for *his* work.

Mildred called them to dinner, and they sat in the big formal dining room. Rick carved the turkey. It was delightful. The conversation was easy and fun. Angelina shook off any traces of shyness in her first ten minutes and babbled away happily to Bobbi. The dog moaned from the back porch. Mildred recalled days gone by. Tracy was so shy around Jason she nearly choked on her food.

After they'd eaten so much that they decided to put off dessert until later, Jason said he had a football in his truck, and he thought they should all go out and play ball to help them digest. "We could let that poor dog out to play with us."

"I'm going to clean up the kitchen," Linda said.

"No, you're not, Mom," Jason informed her. "We need you on the team."

At the back door, everyone else had piled outside, and Linda found herself alone with Tracy. It had not been a mistake. Tracy had waited for this moment.

"I'm sorry," she said softly, "about my sister and your husband."

She didn't elaborate what she was sorry about—the deaths or the affair, but it didn't really matter. Linda saw that there was more to Tracy than timidity. She glimpsed great courage, enough courage to tackle the awkwardness of the situation between them head-on. The girl was hardly older than Bobbi, and yet she was raising her sister's child, and from what Linda could see of it, doing a fine job.

Linda touched Tracy's arm. "Thank you," she said.

Such a small thing, a few seconds, a few words, but a little more of the brittleness fell from Linda's heart.

She and Tracy followed the others outside. The yard was crunchy with leaves, and the fall sunshine streamed, bright, through bare tree branches. Jason had Angelina on his shoulders and picked Linda for his team. That pitted them against Rick and Bobbi and Tracy.

"Oh, I get it," Linda said panting, as she charged across the yard, with the football, Jason running block for her, "you've figured out a way to have all the girls chasing you!"

It truly was hysterical with the dog having no allegiance to anyone and tackling each side with equal vigor. They lost track of who was winning. She could not stop laughing. Rick was outrageously competitive, but even he finally figured out they were never going to know who won. Finally he gave up, and he held out his hand to her. They left the younger ones to play. They checked on Mildred, who was fast asleep on the couch in the living room.

"Want to clean up the kitchen?" she asked him.

"Nah, it'll wait."

Her hand still in his, they sat on the beautiful Wentworth rockers he had put on the side porch. They watched as Jason and the girls and the dog chased around a bit more until they wore out, too. Bobbi took the baby by the hand, and they discovered a leaf pile. Soon their squeals of delight were coming from under heaps of red and orange.

Tracy sat on an old tire swing that Rick had erected.

"When did you find time to do that?" Linda asked him.

"Mildred insisted."

"Humph. I'm surprised."

"Talk to Mildred, she makes all the rules."

She laughed, and looked again at her daughter playing in the leaves with Angelina, at Jason looking down at Tracy with something beautiful and fierce stamped onto the features of his handsome young face. A boisterous snore drifted out of the living room, and she and Rick giggled.

Then time stood still.

Looking at the scene in the yard, feeling Rick's hand reach across and take hers, Linda felt as if a golden light was suffusing the day. Once she had thought her life was shattered. That it was beyond repair, that *she* was beyond repair. But sitting here, enjoying this simplest of moments, something shifted in her.

Was this not exactly the life she had once imagined for herself? Thanksgiving dinners surrounded by family? The shrieks of children? Old people and young people all together? The ebb and the flow of life as present as the flow of the river? Laughter and love and acceptance and hope tingling in the very air? The past and the present and the future all right here in this incredible house, reflected in the gathered wisdom of the old and in the optimism and hopes and dreams of the young?

Angelina erupted from under a pile of leaves, shrieking with delight.

The tears started then, when she saw Bobbi pick up the child—Blair's child, Bobbi's little sister—and lift her over her head, swinging her around. Linda had always dreamed of a sibling for her daughter, had dreamed they might share moments exactly like this one.

This was the miracle then: without all her planning, without her manipulating life to be perfect, what she had always wanted had come to her quietly, through a side door. In the very thing that she thought would destroy her, her husband's infidelity, had been sewn the seeds for this moment, for the life she had today.

A life that included Rick. She looked at this courageous, honest, decent man, and she left her chair and went to his. She sat down on his lap, and tenderly licked her fingers and pressed down the rooster tail that sprang up so wildly on the back his head.

That small gesture felt just as she had known it would: personal and possessive, surprisingly intimate, incredibly right. The tears changed from a trickle to a flood. The walls fell down, and the healing water flowed out from behind them. She cried until his shirt was soaked.

Never once did he ask her to stop. He held her, waiting.

Waiting as he had always waited. As if he had known, all along, even when she didn't know herself, who she really was.

She'd found the missing piece of the puzzle. She knew what she had to do to be worthy of Rick. In her heart, looking at the two beautiful children her husband had given the world, she did the thing that she had thought was impossible. She forgave Blair.

And she forgave herself.

She allowed herself to wonder if all of it—every bit of suffering and humiliation, every bit of painful growth and self-examination—hadn't been for this. To bring her to this very moment where, finally, she could see. Where finally she could open her heart completely to another person. She knew who that other person would be.

Linda opened her heart completely to Rick.

She kissed him as she had wanted to kiss him for so long. Kissed him until she was breathless with it, until a soul that was thirsty, felt filled, until a heart that was broken was mended. She only stopped when she heard a whine.

"Stupid dog," she said affectionately.

"I've decided what to call him," Rick told her softly.

"You have?"

"I'm going to call him Phoenix."

The dog wagged his tail.

"Phoenix," she whispered, and found huge paws in her lap, the dog inserted between her and Rick, licking the tears from her face.

"Phoenix," he repeated firmly, "after the mythical spirit that rises out of ash and destruction, rises stronger, better, a symbol of hope."

"Phoenix," they heard a crabby voice say. "Ridiculous name for a dog."

But the dog, as if he had recognized his name, was already running to Mildred, who had come to stand in the doorway.

"If you two are done making kissy-face," she said sternly, patting the dog when she thought they weren't looking, "we could have some dessert now." Then she smiled.

Linda could not help but notice how her face had changed from their first meeting, softened. Mildred just needed what everybody needed—a place to belong.

That place was called family, but these days, what did that mean? There were first families and second families and even third families. There were ex-husbands and ex-wives. There were stepsisters and brothers and half sisters and brothers. There were people left orphaned by the whole mess. And then there were families of the heart, people drawn together by circumstances and kept together by love.

Perhaps, in the end, these things were better left to heaven.

A long time later, the house was empty, save for Rick and Linda. Jason had driven Tracy and Angelina home, Bobbi had offered to take Mildred home, in her mother's car, and then said she was going to visit an old friend.

"I hope it's not the boy who plays bongo drums," Linda said to Rick, aware of the peace filling the wonderful old house. Aware she had sent her ride away.

"Ah, well, there are probably worse things."

"Such as?"

"Horse thieves. Owners of opium dens. Ax murderers."

She thumped him smartly on the arm, but he took her balled up hand before she could retreat and kissed her knuckles.

"I haven't tried that bathtub yet," he whispered.

"You haven't?" She was aware she was whispering, too.

"No."

"Is that an invitation?" Suddenly she could picture the two of them up there, all the barriers gone, nothing but bubbles.

"Of sorts," he said.

She would thump his arm again if he was going to be obtuse. "Of sorts?"

"I want to share that bathtub with you, Linda, and my bed. This house. My dog. Mildred." He stopped, and then finished quietly, "My life."

"All right," she said. "Should we start with the bath?" She realized she sounded, well, eager.

He chuckled. "Shameless hussy."

All her life she had tried to outrun that label. Now it bounced off her harmlessly because he'd said it with such fondness, as if it wasn't a bad thing at all, as if it was a part of her that he couldn't wait to discover.

Well, she was rather waiting to discover it herself! So his next words disappointed.

"But no, I don't think we should start with the bath."

She hoped that meant he wanted to start with the bed, but she was mistaken.

"I want," he said softly, "to start with the wedding."

And somehow, he had stumbled on the way to start that was just right. She felt it as he wrapped his arms around her. Love. Powerful. Healing. Graceful. Fulfilling. Accepting. Forgiving. She felt it as she had never quite felt it before.

She remembered lying in the September grass, not so long ago, a lifetime ago, trying to discern the message of seeing that rare and beautiful bird, the whooping crane setting his course toward the morning star.

She had known, that morning, that she was being invited to follow his lead, to be greater than she had been up until that point. Her soul had recognized the invitation that had been issued: to expect more of herself, to live with courage, to accept each gift the universe offered her, to dance with freedom.

But all that time, she had thought, it was her turn to be the star chaser.

Now she saw that it was not that at all.

It was her turn not to chase the dream. It was her turn to arrive.

Silhouette

nocturne™

**WAS HE HER SAVIOR
OR HER NIGHTMARE?**

HAUNTED
LISA CHILDS

Years ago, Ariel and her sisters were separated for
their own protection. Now the man who vowed
revenge on her family has resumed the hunt, and
Ariel must warn her sisters before it's too late.
The closer she comes to finding them, the more
secretive her fiancé becomes. Can she trust the man
she plans to spend eternity with? Or has he been
waiting for the perfect moment to destroy her?

On sale December 2006.

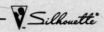

SPECIAL EDITION™

Silhouette Special Edition brings you a
heartwarming new story from the *New York Times*
bestselling author of *McKettrick's Choice*

LINDA LAEL MILLER

Sierra's Homecoming

Sierra's Homecoming
follows the parallel lives
of two McKettrick women,
living their lives in the
same house but
generations apart,
each with a special son
and an unlikely new
romance.

December 2006

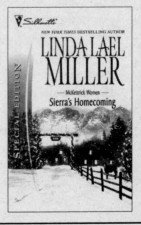

REQUEST YOUR FREE BOOKS!
2 FREE NOVELS PLUS 2
FREE GIFTS!

H A R L E Q U I N   R O M A N C E®

From the Heart, For the Heart

HR06

SILHOUETTE *Romance*®

COMING NEXT MONTH

#1846 IN HER BOSS'S ARMS—Elizabeth Harbison
Laurel Midland is excited about her new job as nanny to a motherless girl with a wealthy but distant father. On her first day, Charles Gray tells her to leave—he wants an older nanny. But Laurel stays, and it isn't long before Charles begins to fall under her spell….

#1847 FALLING FOR THE FRENCHMAN—Claire Baxter
Beth has struggled to get over old love Pierre Laroche, but now he's back, and this time it's to take over her beloved Barossa Valley winery. Beth knows she should hate Pierre, but glimpses of the man she loved ten years ago can still be seen under the cynical businessman….

#1848 HER READY-MADE FAMILY—Jessica Hart
Successful city hotshot Morgan Steele has decided her life is empty—so she gives up her career to move to the country! Handsome neighbor Alistair Brown believes she is a spoiled city girl, but as the attraction between them grows, Morgan realizes he might be everything she's looking for….

#1849 RESCUE AT CRADLE LAKE—Marion Lennox
Top surgeon Fergus Reynard left the city for a GP's life at Cradle Lake, hoping to soothe his broken heart. Ginny Viental is just what he is looking for and Fergus would do anything to make a life with her, even if it means taking on a role he thought he would never face again—that of a father.

SRCNM1206